DREAMERS

A Novel

Graciela Limón

228 Hamilton Ave.,
Palo Alto, CA 94301

To Mary Wilbur, my dearest friend,
who believed in this novel from its beginning.
Thank you, Mary.

AUTHOR'S NOTE

Mothers share memories with their daughters, and so it was that my mother, Altagracia Gómez, shared her sister's story with me. It's a moving account that has stayed with me and inspired the novel you are about to read.

ACKNOWLEDGMENTS

The loving effort of writing *Dreamers* received the help and encouragement of many of my readers and friends, too many to name. However, you know who you are, and to you I owe deep gratitude.

Patricia Oliver, distinguished Professor at Loyola Marymount University, Los Angeles, contributed to *Dreamers* by teaching the novel to her class, "The Rhetoric of Women", even when it was still in manuscript form, which was nothing less than a leap of faith.

And last but not least, I extend my gratitude to Matthew Coleman and his great team at Page Vision Press for the significant editing and artwork that has gone into *Dreamers*.

PROLOGUE

Los Angeles, California, 1932

THEIR DREAM ended one evening late in the year when the V8 Ford climbed the steep hill, gaining speed until it reached the highest point on Whittier Boulevard, just where it abruptly slopes downward. It was there that the car suddenly careened down the hill, moving so fast that startled onlookers froze as it blurred past them, teetering recklessly until its tires got stuck on the streetcar tracks, plunging it downward even faster. When the car reached the bottom of the hill, it was forced upward by a sudden incline, and the driver lost control. The car careened, skidded, flipped, and rolled over once, twice, until it crashed against the curb where it landed on its side.

When the car crashed, only the sound of shattering glass, whirling wheels, and hissing steam escaping from the cracked radiator filled the dusky gloom. Witnesses stood gaping, uncertain of what to do until suddenly, on an impulse, someone broke loose and ran toward the wreckage; others followed. The stranger jumped onto the upturned side of the car and struggled to open the door on the passenger side, but he needed help, and in a panic, he yelled, "Somebody help me!" Then another man came to help pull at the handle, and although they were terrified that the tank might blow, they went on yanking, but the panel was stuck tight; it wouldn't give.

By the time the sound of sirens reached them, others had rushed to help free the trapped couple from that crumpled mass of steel and smoldering rubber. Then someone shouted, "Let's straighten up the thing. Maybe we can open the doors that way!" This time, women ran to join the push, and like ants that move things bigger and heavier than their size, people shoved and heaved until the bashed wreck was put upright.

"Move aside! Make way!"

The police had, by now, come onto the scene, but the crowd was making it hard for the officers to get near the wreckage, and only after pushing his way through the crowd did one of the cops manage to peer into the front seat.

"Smash the window!" It took the other two policemen to break the glass and pry open the door.

The driver was slumped over the wheel; blood from a deep gash on his forehead seeped down his face on to his shirt, but when the officer stuck his head in to get a better look, he shook his head.

"Jesus! The column's nearly chopped him in two." By the driver's side, crumpled against the dashboard was the passenger, a woman. On a closer look, the officer knew right away that she was dead.

"Let's get 'em outta the wreck. Give us a hand! Quick! The engine might blow any minute!"

By that time, an even bigger crowd of babbling, gawking people surrounded the wreck; but a couple of men had the sense to answer the cop's order and helped to drag the bodies out onto the sidewalk. An ambulance arrived, and the orderlies got busy with bandages and other first-aid materials, but then they saw it was too late.

"Christ! What a mess! Looks like the girl died from a broken neck, banged up against the dash, and him, well, the shaft did it."

The officers got busy going through the man's pockets and looking for the woman's purse. They lucked out when IDs were found.

"The guy's name is David Katagian. Hers is Dolores Gómez, and both show the same address over on Vignes. Maybe they were married."

"Or maybe just shacked up," responded the other cop.

"The registration gives another name as the owner of the car. I wonder what's up."

"Can't tell. We can check it out when we get to the precinct."

The officers went on to take statements from witnesses, but there were so many that they stopped when it became clear that the car was going too fast to handle the sudden ups and downs of the street.

"Honest, Officer, I barely caught sight of the car," a woman spoke up with a trembling voice. "It was going so fast it was just a blur."

Another woman, more in control of her nerves said, "It looked almost as if they were doing it on purpose. You know what I mean? Like a joyride, or something crazy like that."

The officer closed his report: "Excessive speed."

Daylight faded into night while the police finished their report and the ambulance headed for the coroner's office. The corner light clicked on, covering the crash scene in an eerie pale light. Evening traffic on the boulevard crawled past the accident as people, curious to see what had happened, slowed down despite the cop's waving arm and irritated shouts to keep moving, to get on their way, to stop the rubbernecking. In the meantime, those bystanders still lingering on the sidewalk were also slow to leave; they wanted to see more. Perhaps it was the sight of where the bodies, shrouded in bloodstained sheets, had been spread out, or maybe it was the mystery of why people do crazy things like driving recklessly. Whatever it was, it held those people spellbound and riveted to the sidewalk.

CHAPTER ONE

A town somewhere in Mexico, 1918

DOLORES GÓMEZ'S journey began when she was eight years old—when she was still a girl with almond-shaped eyes and an olive-complexioned face silhouetted by brown curled hair. She had a lovable disposition back then, with a liking for her mother's caged birds. When she was alone, she hummed while she passed time with schoolwork or drawing. When the next-door kids got together to play with the Gómez children, everyone wanted Dolores to be on their side; she was a good player, never a sore loser, so she was popular.

"She's the most obedient of all," her mother said of Dolores. But some of her aunts could not forget that the girl was born during the year when the Revolution broke out, just when everything wrong with their world happened. They whispered how the girl had come into a life filled with bad signs, killings, and violations, a time filled with omens of worse things to come. The old women felt sorry for the girl, secretly wondering what sadness could be waiting for the child.

But regardless of what the gossipers murmured, Dolores was a sweet-natured cheerful girl, untouched by whatever ugliness had made its way into the world at the time of her birth. That is, she was untainted until a certain day while her father and oldest brother were away, and when Dolores's real journey began.

Toward noon on that day in early November, she was with her brother Héctor, who was twelve, and her sister Altagracia, who was six. They sat on the patio's tiled floor playing a card game. The house was quiet; only the maid moved about finishing last-minute chores before lunch. Close to where the children played, a fountain bubbled; its sounds blended with the chirping of their mother's canaries. It was really the children's hideaway garden where the fragrance of jasmine and honeysuckle filled the air.

It was on that day that Dolores's small world began to fall apart. It started with the slam of the front door followed by agitated footsteps rushing toward them. Out of breath and hardly able to speak, their mother, Cele, followed by her older daughters Pilar and Esperanza, charged in. Dolores did not know it, but it happened that while at the marketplace, a neighbor warned of suspicious strangers hanging around their street.

"Señora Gómez, the intruders are going from house to house, peeping into windows and even trying doors to see which ones are open."

Without uttering a word, Dolores's sisters and mother dropped whatever it was they had bought, desperate to reach their house. When they barged into the patio, their panting and frantic faces scared the children so badly that Altagracia and Héctor jumped up while Dolores froze. No one knew what was happening, and they were confused even more when, without an explanation, their mother ordered, "Dolores, Altagracia! Come with me! Pilar and Esperanza, you too! Quick!"

She took each of the smaller girls by the wrist, nearly dragging them, and at the same time, she glanced over her shoulder and shouted, "Héctor, run to the school! Don't come back until I send for you!"

"But, Mama...!"

The boy didn't have time to finish because his mother and sisters had already disappeared into the rear of the house, heading for a small corral kept for chickens and ducks. Next to that little space was a storage room, a dusty place piled high with empty crates and rusty junk; it was into that place that Cele and her daughters ran.

Once there, she desperately searched, pushing and shoving things until she found a ladder to reach the ceiling and the crawlspace the family called *el tapanco*. She climbed up to the trapdoor, pushing on it hard until it creaked open; she then stuck her head into the dark opening covered with cobwebs. After a few seconds, nearly tripping on her way down, Cele ordered her girls to scramble up. By now, Dolores was really alarmed because she saw her mother's face had turned ashen, and her voice sounded strange; it was hushed and thick.

"Get up there. Quickly! And be quiet!"

When Cele looked at Dolores, the girl caught fear in her mother's eyes, and that terror slipped into Dolores, making her so scared that her stomach churned painfully. But there wasn't time to get sick because in an instant, Cele pushed Altagracia and then Dolores onto the ladder. As soon as the girls disappeared into the gloom, their mother did the same with Pilar and Esperanza. Only then did she scurry up into the space, but then, just as she slammed shut the hatch, she muttered, "*Dios Santo*! The ladder!" She yanked open the door and kicked the ladder out of sight.

When Dolores's eyes adjusted to the dark, she looked around and made out old shovels, rusty rakes, and other trash. Worse still, she realized that they were crowded into a little place with hardly enough headroom for even her smallest sister, Altagracia, to stand upright. They had to crouch on their rumps, all the time panting and trying to hold back tears. But Dolores couldn't help it. She cried, letting out gurgling noises even though she pressed her hand over her nose and mouth. Cele inched closer to her, held a finger on her lips, and at the same time, began to scratch grime off the floorboards. At first, Dolores didn't know what she was doing, but when her mother smeared the gook on Altagracia's face, Dolores understood. "Make yourselves ugly." Cele's voice was barely a whisper, but Pilar and Esperanza heard, and they obeyed.

Beneath them, the house was quiet, and although Dolores was only eight years old, she knew what was happening. She knew of revolutionaries, and federal soldiers too, that hunted for girls and what they did to them once they captured them. Terrified, she sidled even closer to Cele where she would be safe. That's when the screams started up, at first muffled, weak, then louder and filled with terror. Those shrieks were coming from the neighbor's house where Dolores's playmate Dianita and her mother lived. They were terrible cries mixed with men's voices shouting out, laughing and cursing. Although Cele put her hands over Dolores's ears, she could still hear. She heard furniture crashing, breaking glass, and a dog barking; she even heard her friend's terrible cries.

"Mama," she groaned, "they're hurting Dianita. I have to help her!"

Dolores knew she had to do something, so she tried to push away from her mother. She was going to help her friend no matter what happened, but Cele clung to her with such force that the girl could not move.

"Mama, let me go! Please!"

"Dolores, you can't help! No one can."

The girl stopped moving, hoping to fool her mother, and then, just at the right moment, she wrenched away as hard as she could. Because Cele had not expected it, the sudden move stunned her; in that second, Dolores wiggled loose and lunged toward the trapdoor. But before she reached it, Cele sprang, grabbed the girl by the ankles, dragged her back, and pinned her down by wrapping her legs like scissors around Dolores's waist, and holding her like that even though the girl kicked and thrashed. Then after a few moments, still holding tight, her mother stroked the girl's forehead and whispered, "Hush, Dolores! We can't do anything! Only God can help them." Only then did Dolores really stop struggling. But then, something made Esperanza crawl to the trapdoor and put her ear against it. In a moment, her head snapped toward her mother, and she whispered, "They're here!"

Mother and daughters held their breath. Their eyes widened, their ears strained to pick up any sound that told them those men had made their way into the heart of their home. Then rough noises, scrapings on the floor, doors opening and slamming, drawers squeaking, glass shattering, even more terrible sounds moving closer and closer to their hiding place told the women that they had been invaded.

Then the voices seemed to stop just beneath them, cursing and sputtering obscene words. Dolores felt ice fill her belly until it spilled out all the way down her legs, and when she looked down, she saw that she had wet herself. She began to cry because she had not known that being so terrified could make her do such a thing, and she felt ashamed. She thought her sisters would make fun of her if they saw that she was still such a baby, so Dolores glared at them, expecting to catch them laughing at her, but she saw only their faces twisted into masks. She understood that they were terrified too, and that it did not matter that she had peed in her pants. Nothing mattered now.

Minutes dragged by while the shouting went on until a gravelly voice yelled out from another part of the house.

"All right, you pigs! Time to leave! You got enough! Let's go!"

After more yelling and arguing, the women heard the wild cackling and flapping wings of their chickens. They knew those thugs weren't leaving without something in their sacks; this time, it would be at least chickens. At last the squawking finally faded into an eerie silence almost as scary as the screams and racket. It was the quiet that comes before something terrible, so the women crouched against one another, tense and waiting. They stayed there for a long time, hardly breathing.

"I'm going down. All of you stay here until I tell you it's safe."

Cele got to her knees and wrenched open the trapdoor. She took a few seconds to look into each of her daughters' eyes, letting them know that she expected them to obey her.

"But, Mama, the ladder isn't there anymore. You kicked it out of the way. How will you get down there without hurting yourself?"

Cele blinked hard and then poked her head down through the opening to scan the space below, all the time searching for a way to get down. She wagged her head.

"I can do it."

Although she mumbled, the girls made out her words but didn't understand how she was going to get down without hurting herself. While they were trying to make sense of what their mother planned to do, she pulled her skirt up, bound it around her waist, swung her legs down through the opening, grabbed onto an edge, and then eased herself down until she dangled in midair.

"Mama!"

Cele moved so quickly that even as the girls tried to hold onto her, she had already swung her body downward, let go, and landed on a pile of crates. When she tumbled off the stack, she took a few seconds to catch her breath and then got to her feet. Cele looked up at her daughters' faces peering down at her and shot up a shaky grin. "I'm well."

Cele was covered in dust. Her face was smudged with grime; her hair had come loose from its bun and clung to her neck and shoulders. As she made her way toward the ladder that had landed behind some junk, she loosened her skirt and patted the dust off her shoulders and arms. Suddenly, a pair of hands sprang out from behind, grabbed her by the nape of her neck, and at the same time, yanked her hair, and brought her down flat on the floor. Then the attacker was on top of her. With one hand, he ripped away at Cele's blouse and clawed at her skirt until her legs were exposed, all the while he struggled to pull down his pants with the other hand.

For an instant, Cele was stunned, but then she lashed back, thrashing and screaming. She sunk her teeth into the man's hand and arm so hard that he pulled back and slapped her hard. But then she reached up to dig her nails into his grimy cheeks, and she yanked at his head so hard that his sombrero flew off, exposing a mop of tangled, dirty hair. Cele grunted as she shoved her knee into his groin, over and over, fierce and hard, once landing on his already exposed penis.

"Ay!"

He groaned, but although the blow slowed him down, it did not knock him off her. It only forced him to pause to regain his breath. In the meantime, the panicked girls looked down from their perch, gaping at the heaving backside of their mother's attacker. They saw he was mauling her, already inside of her, heaving and thumping, but she was fighting back with her knees, shoving hard against those ugly buttocks.

In seconds, Cele's daughters realized they couldn't watch their mother's rape without doing something. Pilar was the first to jump through the opening just as her mother had done. Esperanza followed her, and then Dolores. Only Altagracia stayed behind; she was too little and too scared to fling herself down into that hole.

The girls, shrieking like wild animals, leaped down onto the ruble, and from there, like a flock of cawing furious birds, landed on the man's back so hard that his backbone buckled, making him flop onto his side, unnerved and utterly confused. Liberated, Cele got out from under him, got on her feet, and together with her daughters, kicked, pummeled, and punched the rapist, each one striking with all the might in her arms and legs while the man struggled to defend himself. He tried to shield his groin with one hand and to fend off his attackers with the other, but he was so shaken all he could do was grunt and jiggle his legs in the air until one of his huaraches come loose and skidded across the floor.

He finally managed to roll over onto his belly and slither away from the pounding, using his elbows like paddles. His raggedy trousers hung off his buttocks, making movement more difficult, but because he was panic-stricken, he crawled and groveled until he escaped from what he thought were vultures that had swooped down from somewhere above. The women, stunned, panting, and crying bitter tears of rage, glared at the good-for-nothing as he slithered away; but it was Pilar who snapped out of that trance and frantically thrashed around, looking for something, anything, to kill him. When she caught sight of a pitchfork sticking out from under a pile of dirty rags, she grabbed it and lunged toward the rapist until she stood over him. Then she plunged the thing deep between shoulder blades, lungs, and heart; she did it over and over. It was a quiet act. Only a deep wind escaped through the man's clenched jaws. Then there was stillness, until Cele staggered to her trembling daughter.

"Stop, Pilar! It's done."

Cele pried the weapon out of her daughter's hands and threw it aside while trying to calm her. She took time to catch some breath because she, too, was still trembling hard. Then she turned to her other daughters.

"Come! We have to do away with him."

CHAPTER TWO

An orphanage somewhere in Lebanon, 1918

DAVID KATAGIAN'S journey began nearly on the same day when Dolores, in her corner of the world, cringed in *el tapanco* with her mother and sisters. On that day, the thirteen-year-old orphan crouched against a crumbling brick wall, his emaciated arms holding his knees tight against his chest; his hands bruised and filthy. His body, covered by a ragged uniform, was bony; it ached all over, but what hurt most of all was his bruised scalp that was shaved and scrubbed with disinfectant every week.

He wasn't the only orphan in that place. The courtyard where he found myself on that day was vast; it was filled with a milling crowd of boys just as wasted and tattered as he was. Empty-eyed and silent, they wandered around the yard like hungry hounds sniffing the ground for something to eat. David couldn't tell how many boys there were, maybe hundreds, maybe more, and all of them were the same in one way.

In 1915, the Ottoman Turks had forced those boys to witness their fathers dragged away. "To help in the war against our enemies," they said. But those boys knew it was a lie, that it was a death sentence, and that their fathers would never return.

After David's father was taken, his family was forced to march south over treacherous mountains and then down across the Syrian Desert until they reached the ocean. The few elders unlucky enough to survive the ordeal were crammed into camps where they died miserably. The children that lived were crowded into the orphanages like the one where David lived for more than three years. It was a wretched time for him, empty and brutal, with nothing to relieve the ugliness of pain and hunger except the memory of his family.

As if their names had been fresh air, he spent hours breathing their names in and out, and this much no Turk could take away from him because his thoughts were his secret. He clung to them and to the memories of his family's farm outside of Sivas in Old Armenia where the Katagian clan made a living cultivating orchards and tending herds.

David spent most of his time at the orphanage remembering, until one day, he realized that some of his memories were beginning to fade, so he forced himself to repeat those recollections in his mind so as not to forget them. Whenever he was alone, he forced his mind off his Turk overseers and his growling belly.

All David had to do was close his eyes to relive how his uncles and cousins, on days off work, spread blankets by the riverbank where they laid out food to eat. Food! That was where his thoughts stopped to think of the fruit, vegetables, meat, bread, and delicious candy. Oh, how his stomach yearned for just a few bites, even a lick. He regretted the times he had turned up his nose at this piece of meat or that other vegetable, getting his mother to scold him. "This is good food! Eat! One day you won't have it, and then you'll be sorry!" He had been a spoiled boy, and now he was sorry, just as his mother warned.

David liked to remember how his mother and youngest uncle made music for the enjoyment of everyone on those days by the riverbank. She strummed her guitar, and he blew wistful notes from his flute, the instrument that imitated the sound of rustling leaves. There in the middle of the grayness and stink of the orphanage, the boy remembered the music, its lilting harmony echoed in his ears. But whenever he crouched out of sight, dreaming, one of the teachers, a Turk like the others, inevitably crept up on him and lashed him hard with a switch.

Swish! Along with the hissing sound of that dreaded weapon came the stinging pain, and the cursing.

"Stinking maggot! Get off your ass and get to work! Stop being the son of the infected female pig that incubated you!"

David detested the Turks, but he hated the switch almost as much. It was the instrument used to flog the boys' bare feet, especially on the sole, where it hurt the most. It was the Turks' favorite punishment, and the one most feared, almost as much as being kept from the day's ration of stale bread and thin soup.

After his father and uncles were kidnapped, leaving only David's mother and grandmother to defend their home, the house was looted. "We're looking for rifles and pistols," said the Turks, but it was a stupid excuse no one believed.

David's mother and grandmother were told to pack food and whatever they could carry because their family was going to be moved. "For your safety." Again, the Turks lied. The worst part was that the Katagian family wasn't the only one to be pushed out of their home. From David's village alone, dozens of other women and children were herded together, and like cattle, they were prodded onward on that death march. A few days later, when their food and water ran out, people began to starve while the Turks pushed the trek forward, all the time insulting and beating them.

The prisoners walked for days until their shoes wore out and fell off their feet, and those that collapsed from pain or thirst were clubbed until they died. All the time, David's mother urged Melik, his older brother, to take care of David, just as she was taking care of their baby sister, Arpi, as well as their grandmother.

No one was allowed to stop except for short times during the day, and at night to sleep. It was only because of the pity of strangers that brought the prisoners bread and water that they survived. The sun blazed without letup, forcing even more people to collapse and die by the wayside.

The worst suffering happened when the women were forced to strip naked and go to the rear of the line. All the time, the guards jeered and howled lewd words while lashing them with tree branches. Those women obeyed until they fainted or dropped dead, covered only by humiliation and shame.

David did not see that terrible thing happen to his mother because Melik tore off a piece of his shirt, and blindfolded him. But David knew what was happening. He saw it happen to other women, so he knew his mother was murdered in a shameful cruel way, and no matter how tight his brother wrapped up his eyes, David felt her pain and humiliation.

He never forgot that terrible death, but in a mysterious way, it was a good thing because it planted a deep hatred in him, and it was that loathing that saved his life once he was imprisoned in the orphanage. It was that intense fire stuck deep in his belly that gave the boy the guts to survive, and even to kill. He survived not only because of hatred, but because he wanted to live, and this feeling was so strong it kept him alive, even when he was forced to watch his brother starve to death.

After his brother and mother died, David changed. He wasn't a boy anymore, and what happened afterward could not have surprised anyone. One of the orphanage overseers, a Turk whose name David never learned, began to visit him at night when the other boys were asleep. The first time, the man crept out of the darkness like a shadow holding a piece of bread in his hand. And David was so hungry that without asking why the guard was being kind, the boy snatched the crust and gulped it down.

That was all the Turk did that time. He did not speak or ask anything; he just sat with David, and then he disappeared back into the darkness as slyly as he had appeared. But then, it happened again; the silent man with bread in his hand appeared out of the gloom. It went on for nights until the man made his move; it happened just when David was on the verge of trusting him. He touched him! Startled and frightened, he pushed the man away, and although the rejection worked, it wasn't for long. The Turk backed away that first time, but he returned night after night afterward to give David even more pain and shame.

David slept in a bed with three other boys, so the Turk snatched and carried him to a corner where he pulled down his pants and did dirty things to him. But it wasn't easy because David kicked and scratched the Turk's face, but when he tried to scream, the man pressed his wet mouth on the boy's so he couldn't let out a sound. Each time the attack went on until the Turk had his satisfaction, grunted, and then loosened his grip on David, dragged him back to the bed and hissed, "Keep your mouth shut, or I'll kill you!" And because David believed him, he did not tell anyone. He kept the feeling of filthiness locked up inside and passed the first day as if in a nightmare, afraid that it would happen again when nighttime came.

And it did. It happened every night, so many times that David couldn't remember for how long. Weeks? Months? It lasted until he became so sick with disgust that he knew he had to do something.

Then it happened! When the idea first came to David that he had to stop what the Turk was doing, he felt a strange feeling come over him. Just thinking that he could be rid of that disgusting pig made him strong.

He asked himself what he could do knowing that if he went to someone for help he wouldn't be believed, or worse, the Turk would find out and kill him. After each assault, David hardly slept at night, thinking, planning, and during the day, he searched for a way out until he got it! He decided to follow the Turk to see where he went, and what he did after he was finished with him.

One night, David followed the man and crept behind him, sneaky, nearly invisible, all the time melting into the shadows of the long passageways that led to where the Turk slept. David saw that he stopped at a big window, opened it wide, and sat on its ledge to smoke a cigarette while he leaned back, his body loose and relaxed while he gazed up at the sky, puffing. Each suck he took made the end of the butt glow bright enough to throw a reflection on his flabby face; all the time David glared at him so hard he felt his eyeballs bulging. The Turk stayed there for a long time while David spied on him, watching his every move, looking at how he fondled himself between his legs as if still feeling what he had done. Later on, David discovered the attacker did this every time; it was a routine.

That was the first time, but David followed the Turk every night after that, all the time trying to find a way to get rid of that devil. Of all the ideas that came to him, only one stuck: The Turk was weakest while he sat at the open window.

The boys' dormitory was on the third floor of the building, making it a straight fall onto a stone pavement below the window where the Turk squatted. There was nothing to break his fall, nothing for him to grab to save himself. All David had to do, he told himself, was creep up and push. It did not matter that the man was big, and he just a small boy;

all he had to do was shove when the Turk was gazing up at the stars, squeezing more pleasure out of himself. That's when his balance was off.

It was a good plan, but something held David back. He knew he was afraid, but there was more than just being a coward. What was it? Was it Satan protecting the Turk, or was it David's angel keeping him from a sinful act? Whatever it was, a voice repeated over and again that to kill a human is murder, a mortal sin. Did not his mother as well as their priest always teach him that to commit such a sin meant going to hell? Did not murder make the murderer just as evil as the one he killed?

While David tried to find the answer to that riddle, he lost nights hesitating. All the time, the Turk returned to do his thing until the boy finally made up his mind. He put aside thinking about mortal sin and hell because he couldn't stand the Turk's sour breath on his neck anymore, much less his dirty hands on his body. If he was going to hell, well then, there was no way out of it. David chose hell.

That night, David followed the Turk to his window, watching him hoist his rump onto the ledge. As if pasted to the wall, the boy slithered toward him in the dark, one small step at a time, patiently waiting for just the right moment. His eyes, used to the darkness, watched the man take deep drags on the cigarette while massaging his crotch and gazing at the stars as if thanking them for so much pleasure.

Then David lunged! Arms outstretched rigid and straight, the palms of his hands held up stiff like shields. He charged and rammed the man's shoulder with all his strength. The Turk didn't have a chance to yelp or scream, and in less than a second, David heard the hollow flop of meat and bones on the pavement below. It was a good sound! He didn't even look to see what was left of that detestable thing; he just returned to the tiny wedge of bed that was his, and he fell asleep.

For some days, he saw on the faces of other boys a look of relief, even joy, when they heard of the Turk's death. It was then he knew that he had not been the only one, and so David Katagian came out of the killing uncharged and unpunished and liberated. At first there was a fuss over the Turk's death, but when it became clear that he had accidentally fallen out the window, the event was soon forgotten.

CHAPTER THREE

Mexico

DOLORES DIDN'T have David's ability to find escape after a death. Her nature was different. Killing the rapist did not erase the wretchedness he had caused; instead, her anguish intensified, mostly because she was unable to understand what had happened that day.

The ordeal transformed her. The horror of her playmate's screams, the rape of her mother, and the killing of the man burned deep into her consciousness where it stayed, stuck somewhere behind her eyeballs and down deep in her chest. Dolores aged as she, her mother, and sisters toiled through that long night, digging a pit, and then as she witnessed flinging the lifeless carcass into that hole. Each shovel-full plunged her deeper into a cloudy in-between world where she was neither girl nor woman.

Cele was aware of Dolores's anguish, even as she also sensed her other daughters' shock and turmoil; but since she, too, was trapped in the aftermath of that ordeal, she needed time to draw from within her spirit the strength to free her daughters from the darkness that had overtaken them. It wasn't too long afterward that Cele called them to her side where they met in a secluded room of the house.

"I know, daughters, the pain you're feeling, so I will speak of what happened just this one time, but never again. I ask you to listen to me carefully."

Mother and daughters stood in a tight circle, so close that elbows touched. Dolores put her arms around her mother's waist and leaned her head on her breast.

Cele peered into each girl's eyes, waiting for someone to say something, but they kept quiet, so she went on. "What we did was in our defense."

One voice, it seemed, answered, "Yes, Mama."

"We did nothing wrong! The man violated me, and by doing that, he soiled each of you. You were as defiled as I was, and there wasn't anything else to do but what we did."

It was Dolores who blurted out, "I'm so ashamed," and tears muffled her words.

"No, you must not be ashamed! We must not be ashamed! The shame is on the man!"

"But Pilar killed him! What will happen to us? Won't we be punished?"

Avoiding Dolores's question, Cele turned to Pilar. "And even if it was you, daughter, who put an end to him, it was as if each of us had plunged the sharp blades into him. We all did it! Hear me, Dolores! Each one of us is responsible but only because it was in our defense. We cannot ever forget that! What we did was not wrong! We won't be punished!"

In her intense desire to wipe out any trace of guilt in her girls, Cele's voice had grown low and raspy, "One more thing! We must now promise to keep what we did a secret. No one is ever to know what we did, or where we buried the criminal." She turned again to Dolores, "If we keep the secret no one will know, and if no one knows, we won't be punished."

"Not even Papa?"

This time, it was Esperanza who broke in.

"I'll speak with your father. But only me, no one else!"

"Yes, Mama!"

"Each one of us will swear now to keep what we did a secret. Pilar, swear!"

The daughter that had killed the man, and visibly the most shaken, uttered the words, "I swear, Mama."

Then Cele turned to Esperanza. "I swear," uttered the girl.

Dolores mumbled, "I swear!" But after a short pause, she blurted out, "What about Altagracia? She was there too, wasn't she?"

"No, daughter. She was not a witness to anything, so never, never say anything to her."

Mother and daughters then huddled for a time in stunned silence, knowing they had done something that put them on a new path. Their secret, even if unspoken, would forever fill the space between them. It could be said that mother and daughters had become one.

After that, days felt long, dreary, and all wrong, unpredictable; everyone was jumpy and irritable. Dolores and the other children bickered. The younger ones did not play much anymore, especially since she, before playful and feisty, was now gloomy and sulky. She was sad, and she showed it; she seemed to hate everything and would not speak, and she hardly ate.

No one imagined that at nighttime, when she was in bed, the screaming and crying that happened that day came back to her no matter how hard she clasped her hands over her ears. Every night, she saw her mother's face in the darkness and the image of Pilar's upraised arms clutching the pitchfork. More than anything, Dolores was haunted by the words, "I swear, Mama! I swear!"

These images haunted Dolores for years until they began to diminish and fade, until her life reached its full circle.

CHAPTER FOUR

Lebanon

IT WAS about that time that the Great War ended, and the Ottoman Turks went on the run, leaving behind the orphanage in shambles. Boys, teachers, guards, cooks, nurses, all scattered, disoriented, and scared, not knowing who was in charge or what they were supposed to do; all anyone knew was that they had to escape.

David Katagian was now free to leave the place where he had known so much pain, yet he was afraid to venture out by himself. Like the rest, he felt lost and confused; he did not know what to do, so on that day, he stood in a stupor, staring at the babbling, panic-stricken crowd scrambling around him. Paralyzed, he stayed there until he remembered an out-of-the-way corner on the far side of the orphanage where he could hide. He ran to the place, and there he huddled out of sight, watching people doing whatever they could to save themselves.

From a distance, David watched men shove helpless orphans aside just to steal their place on trucks or passing carts. Where was their shame? David did not have the answer, but neither did he have the courage to step up to help anyone, so he shrunk back into his hole and waited to see what happened next. But after a while, he wondered what it was he was waiting for; he did not know the answer to that question either.

He thought of his life at the orphanage, and although it had been a place of torment, hadn't he somehow managed to survive? He even murdered a man there. He quickly pushed aside that old feeling of guilt and, instead, concentrated on how he had become so accustomed to the orphanage that its rooms and walls had even come to give him a strange sense of safety. In a curious way, having to leave that hated place now scared him, yet he could see that the orphanage was falling apart; there was no way for him to stay.

More frightening thoughts churned in his mind as he shrank into the hideaway, wishing he could stay there forever, even though he knew it was impossible. For the time being, however, he decided to sleep and wait for something to happen. He slept deeply, but when it became night, the temperature turned bitterly cold. His threadbare uniform and worn-out shoes barely helped, and although he hugged his knees, trying to get warm, he still felt himself getting colder. He rubbed his head hard, trying to heat his scalp, but when it grew numb with cold no matter how much he rubbed, he knew he had to do something. Putting aside his terror of being captured, he sucked in a deep breath, and only then did he creep away from that hideaway.

He slithered out, wishing he could melt into a wall, or maybe become invisible by slipping behind those stone pillars. When he finally reached the gate leading out of the compound, he sprinted through it, expecting a stinking Turk to grab him by the neck, but nothing happened. No one even noticed the boy was escaping; there were too many people doing the same thing.

It was early morning now, yet the same agitated commotion of the day before was still going on, making it hard for David to find someone to ask how to get a place on a truck, or in what direction to go. Every time he tried, he was pushed away or insulted.

"Move away, pig face!"

"Who are you, mongrel?" Shouts and insults were hurled at the boy until he gave up trying; he stopped where he was, crossed his arms, deciding to stay where he was, and waited. What was he waiting for? He didn't know, but at least he wasn't as scared anymore, so now he stood in the middle of that crazy mob for a long time, looking around while he was pushed and cursed.

As if anchored to the ground, David did not leave that spot until he finally made out an old woman sitting under a tree on the fringe of the crowd. He couldn't tell what it was about her that got his attention. Maybe it was the frayed shawl that covered her head, or it could have been her wrinkled face, or her hunched-over body that seemed oblivious to the calamity whirling around her. Whatever it was, David stared at her until he noticed that she gestured for him to come to her. He was surprised at first, doubting her signal was aimed at him, but when she nodded, letting him know it was he whom she wanted, he pushed his way through the crowd until he reached her, and then crouched on the ground next to her.

Up close, David saw that she was even older than he had thought; she was wrinkled, toothless, and one eye was filmy gray, like that of a fish; but she had a smile that was sweet and gentle.

"Hello," she said.

"Hello," he stuttered.

Without saying more, the old woman reached into a sack that was at her side and came up with a piece of bread.

"Take it, son. Eat!"

David grabbed the crust, but his hand shook so much he could hardly put the morsel into his mouth. He did not think of thanking her, much less did he ask why she was sharing that precious bread; all that mattered was that his belly ached for that morsel. As he gobbled and gulped, the old woman handed him a little jug of water, and the boy drank deeply; only then did he stop shaking.

He stared at the woman, wondering if he was dreaming, or if she was a spirit his mind was making up to play a trick on him. But when he looked down at his hand and saw leftover crumbs on his fingers, and when he felt drops of water that had dripped off his chin onto his chest, he thought, *No, she's not a ghost.*

The old woman and boy sat for a long time staring at one another, communicating in silence, and David sensed that she was making up her mind about him. She must have been wondering about his age and even judging his looks. He was fourteen, but after so much starvation and bad treatment, he was scrawny and short for his age; only the thin fuzz covering his upper lip hinted at his real age. His skin was sallow, and his eyes once bright had lost their light; only his hair, now beginning to grow back was thick and so dark brown it looked black under certain light.

The old woman is looking at me trying to know something about me. Thinking this, David stared back, wanting to discover something he had not seen before, but there was nothing. The more he glared at her, the more he liked her because, strangely, she made him feel safe. Just then, the old woman broke into his thoughts; her voice was thin but firm.

"My name is Zepyur. What is your name?"

Still a little nervous, David said, "I'm David Katagian from the town of Sivas in Old Armenia. And you, Old One, where are you from?"

"Oh, that's difficult to say."

"Why?"

"Because I'm from so many places that I cannot tell exactly where I began life. My mother, I know, was Egyptian, a descendant of the Coptic people, and my father was a merchant from Cypress who made his livelihood traveling from place to place selling herbs and medicines and precious counsel. I was born somewhere along the many routes they took through empires and villages, so I cannot tell exactly where I was born. It could have been anywhere."

The boy was baffled by what she was saying, and he wrinkled his brow. He listened intently as Zepyur spoke, amazed that she did not know where she had been born.

"What's your family's name?"

"I don't know that either."

"Yet your first name is Armenian. Could it be that you were born in Old Armenia, and that maybe you have an Armenian family name?"

"Is my name Armenian? I didn't know that, but if you say so, then it must be. Zepyur is what I've always been called, nothing more, and perhaps it's true that I was born in Old Armenia. Who knows?"

Again, they became quiet. David was intrigued by the old woman's calm way of speaking, as well as her casual manner with something so serious and important as her ancestry. He was thinking of his own name, his ancestors, and the place where he was born. Then it occurred to him to ask more.

"Why did you call me from among so many other people?"

"Because you're going to be my guide. As you can see, one of my eyes is useless, which means I can hardly see, and that I need help to get to where I'm going."

Now David was really puzzled, and just to be sure, he moved closer to Zepyur to take a better look at her bad eye. Then he twisted around to look back toward where he had been standing when she called.

"I don't understand. How were you able to see me from so far away if you can't see?"

"Oh, that's easy to explain. I saw you clearly because there's a special light around you."

"A light?"

"Yes! But you're not the only one. There have been other people in my life that share your light. Some people have it, and some do not." She paused, and then she repeated, "Will you be my guide?"

"Yes, but you must tell me where we're going. I'm lost, and I don't know where to go, much less how to get to where you're going."

"I'll tell you where to go."

Zepyur stopped speaking to rummage for something in her satchel until she found what she was looking for. It was a coat.

"In the meantime, here's this coat for your shoulders. It will keep you warm."

"Thank you!" he murmured as he slipped the cover around his shoulders, buttoned it at his neck, and right away, he felt heat spread onto his shoulders and down to the rest of his body.

"Now, it's time for us to begin our journey, but first, get nearer to me so that I may bless you."

Wordlessly, the boy shuffled as close as he could to the old woman and lowered his head. He felt her frail hands on his grimy hair as she uttered words that were as whispery and soft as her touch.

"David Katagian, I bless you now and forever! May the angels be your protectors and guides!"

David felt a strange sensation come over him. He felt that never again would he suffer the pain and fear he had experienced at the orphanage as long as Zepyur's blessing was with him, and he was so moved he had trouble speaking, until he finally squeezed out a few words.

"Where will we go, Old One?"

She raised her hand and pointed a bony finger toward the setting sun.

"We'll go in that direction."

"What will we find there?"

"Constantinople."

CHAPTER FIVE

Mexico

AFTER THE calamity, Cele Gómez knew she had to tell her husband what happened, but she sensed that Ignacio was already on the edge of darkness himself. She was afraid of how he would react if he knew the whole truth—that she and her daughters had killed one of those misfits, and that his body was buried just a few feet from where they sat at that moment. She decided instead to tell only part of what happened, the part of the break-in.

"It's my fault," he murmured when she finished telling him.

"Why? Those animals are on the loose everywhere."

"People know that I'm against the uprisings."

"How do they know?"

"Because I speak out against them whenever I can."

"Oh!"

"They want to get even, and it's only going to get worse. I know they will come back unless I go away."

"What do you mean?"

"I must leave, Cele."

"All of us?"

"No, just Sebastián and me. I'll send for you and the children when I find where we can settle."

"Where would you go?"

"To the other side of the border."

She was stunned, but she quickly put together what she was hearing. "These aren't new thoughts, are they?"

"No. I've been planning."

Her mind raced, and in moments, she saw that if Ignacio disappeared, it would draw attention from the scene of the killing; it would cast him as the probable culprit.

She wondered, *Would this not be the solution?* So she asked, "Is there no other way?"

"No."

She retreated into thought, and after a while, convinced that her husband's plan was best, Cele pushed aside any feelings of guilt.

That night, Cele and Ignacio Gómez sat at table surrounded by their children; there was a stiff feeling in the room. The family was in a glum mood; no one spoke, no one laughed. There was something like a lingering cloud that hung over them. The only sound was the ticking of a clock on a side cabinet. Now and then, someone let out a little cough.

Altagracia, Héctor, and Dolores did not know what was happening, but they guessed that Sebastián, their older brother, knew, so they stared at him hoping to get something from his expression; but he fidgeted with a napkin, his face a blank. Sebastián, dark-skinned with the sensitive features inherited from his mother, was nineteen years old, and mature beyond his age, knew what was about to happen, but he didn't let on. On that night, no matter how much the kids stared at him, they couldn't make out anything that might tell them what was going on.

After a while, Dolores looked over at Pilar and wondered if what was happening had anything to do with their secret, but her sister was concentrating on rubbing something off the tablecloth, her face nearly hidden with an expression that said nothing. Then Dolores stared at Esperanza, her eyes showed how anxious she was to understand the reason for so much gloom, but Esperanza shrugged, frightening Dolores even more, and making her think that maybe the dead man's comrades had come looking for him.

Then the girl stared at her mother but saw that she sat with eyes half closed, waiting for her husband to say something, so Dolores turned to look at her father. Now she really felt uneasy, afraid, because his expression showed what she had not seen before. It was as if a cloud covered his face, and his eyes were sunk into dark circles. He finally cleared his throat, but when he spoke, his voice was scratchy, different. Everyone tensed because they couldn't remember a time when their father had spoken that way.

"Your mother and I have something important to tell you tonight."

Sebastián and Héctor sat up, wondering what could be so serious; at the same time, the girls felt certain that what they had done was discovered. Tense, they waited, yet he said nothing. Instead, he seemed out of breath, as if something were caught in his throat. The clock's ticking got louder while the shadows on his face got worse, but still, he did not speak. Cele, seeing that she had to take over, spoke up; she was blunt, not even trying to soften what she knew would upset them.

"Tomorrow, your father and Sebastián will leave."

At first, the family was quiet, but then, a din of squeaking chairs, thrashing arms, and a torrent of questions broke out. Only Sebastián and Pilar, eyes still pasted on the tablecloth, kept still. Cele waited for the racket to stop before speaking.

"Your father and brother are leaving because they can't stay here."

"Why?"

"Because it's too dangerous."

"Why?"

"I'll explain later, Héctor."

"Where are they going?"

"They're going up north where they will wait for us."

"Mama, are we going too?"

"Yes, Dolores, in time, all of us we'll follow."

Cele glanced at Ignacio, but since he still kept silent, she said, "For now, that's all your father and I have to say." Then she looked around the table and sighed deeply. "It's time for all of you to go to bed. I'll come in a while to pray with you."

Confused, everyone, even her husband, shuffled out of the room while Cele stayed in her place lost in thought. With a last glance, Dolores saw how her mother held her plump hands clasped on her lap; she looked calm, but those twitching fingers betrayed anxiety. The girl did not want to leave; she needed to know what was happening, so she tiptoed behind the door where she hid unnoticed yet able to overhear everything.

Cele felt tormented and knew she had to open her heart to someone, so she decided to speak to Sebastián who always gave her strength.

"Sebastián, stay for a few minutes."

His mother's voice made him pause then look around, making Dolores freeze, convinced that he caught her hiding right there behind the door. But no, he just turned and moved over to the seat next to his mother where he sat close up to her; their faces pale in the blue-gray gaslight, making them look older than their age.

After some moments, Sebastián slipped even closer to Cele, took one of her hands, and leaned his head on her shoulder. It was not unusual for him to show his affection that way; he had done it since he was a boy. When they spoke, their voices were hushed, nearly whispers, making Dolores strain to hear.

"Mama, don't be afraid."

"I am afraid, but I'm even sadder, and my heart is breaking."

Sebastián was startled by the sadness in his mother's voice and words, so he pulled away to look into her eyes.

"Papa will be safe, I promise you. Leave that to me. Just because I'm young doesn't mean I don't know what to do in case of trouble, and I'm strong."

Cele smiled as she pulled his head back onto her shoulder and then waited a few moments before speaking. Maybe she wanted more time to feel Sebastian's affection.

"I know that you will keep your father safe. But there's more that makes me afraid."

Cele had no intention of revealing to Sebastián the truth about the killing; it would be too great a burden, just as it would have been for her husband. Nonetheless, she had to speak.

"What is it?"

"It's about all of us. What if we fall apart as a family?"

"What makes you say that?"

"I feel it, Sebastián, here in my heart. Our roots are here, in this house, and it's slipping away from us."

"I don't see it that way, Mama." He sat up abruptly. "This house is just a house, and I promise you that we can find another one just as strong and beautiful as this one once we decide where we want to settle."

"Maybe. But what if it doesn't happen that way, and we're left without shelter, without a place to call home? Some people are forced to wander the streets without a roof to cover them in times of need. I'm so afraid of such a calamity."

Cele, in an effort to keep her turmoil to herself, spoke with eyes nearly closed, but her lips betrayed deep anxiety, letting Sebastián know she did not share his confidence in their future. He saw she was really afraid.

"Please don't think that way. Papa and I will first of all find work and then get a house for all of us to live in. Then will you and the children follow."

She sighed; she wanted to share his way of thinking, but there was much more that weighed upon her that she could not share, so she digressed.

"What about our loved ones who have passed and gone on to the other life?"

"What about them?"

"Here on this piece of earth is where they were born. Here is where their bones are buried, where we often visit them. We'll abandon our departed when we leave, won't we?"

Sebastián was struck by the thought of leaving behind his ancestors. He had not thought of it; he didn't know what to say, so he kept quiet for a time until Cele broke in.

"There's something else. It's about your father."

"Mama, I already said that I'll be at his side always. He won't be in danger."

"There's more than just his safety."

"What do you mean?"

Without thinking, she brought up something she only half kept on her mind. "I'm afraid your father is in danger of losing his place as the head of our family."

"I don't understand what you mean." Sebastián was taken off guard. "Why should that happen? I know that he has to leave, but he'll always be himself, our father, our *jefe*. Nothing will change except the place where we come together, and then everything will be the same. Mama, the only difference will be that everything will be newer, and we'll have opportunities in that new life we don't have here. No more war, or drunken soldiers, or stinking bodies hanging from trees. They say it's wonderful up there on the other side. I think that I'm going to like it, and I want you to like it."

Cele pulled away to look at him. "You're young," and then she brought him closer. "But think of it, Sebastián, he's being forced to give up his place here where he's lived all of his life. Up there, he'll be a stranger among other strangers, all of them rootless and drifting. As for us, we will be left alone, a family without a head, and he's bound to feel that deeply."

"He'll have me to remind him of his place."

"You're a beautiful son." Cele paused for a few moments and then shook her head as if trying to get rid of bad thoughts. She even put on a little smile. "I wasn't thinking right." She stopped speaking. Sebastián waited for her to go on, but she kept quiet.

"There's something else on your mind, isn't there?"

Cele almost blurted out what she and his sisters had done but again found something else to say.

"Your father has never worked with his hands. He's a man used to providing for himself and his family in commerce. I don't think it will be like that for him up there."

"We'll find a way, I promise you. In the beginning, it's going to be hard, and I think he will find it harder than I will, but when you and the children join us it will be better."

"Sebastián, you don't understand! Your father is being forced by enemies to change his way of life. People hate him and have even threatened his life. He's been forced to endure the insult of the assault here on our home. Think of it! This has robbed him of much of his dignity."

"Mama, I don't understand you." Now Sebastián was really baffled. "Papa will always be himself."

"Maybe you're right, son. I'm certain of one thing, however, and that is that our life as a family will change. We've never been separated, and I'm afraid we're in danger of breaking up."

Sebastián was now feeling a growing irritation because of so many worries being pushed onto him. Cele noticed and tried to change the subject.

"And what about your sisters? What will their lives be like up there in that strange world? Will they be transformed? Some of my friends know of one or two of our own young women that have returned from up there, and they say those women have come back so changed their families hardly recognize them. Those women talk and dress differently, and worst of all, they're filled with terrible, shameless ideas."

Sebastián wanted to laugh, but when he caught his mother's expression, he knew she was really afraid for his sisters' future. He felt a tinge of shame.

"Mama, that's only gossip. Don't listen to what those old hags say. What do they know? Why should my sisters change? I think life will be better. They will love it up there."

Despite what he was saying, Sebastián began to feel dejected because he pictured his sisters grown up, dressed like gringas, and maybe even talking in the strange language they talk up there on the other side of the border. He felt his excitement melt away; instead, dejection crept in even though he tried to fight it off.

"Why is this happening to us, Mama?"

"Your father couldn't hold his tongue, and he accused the revolutionaries to their faces of terrible things."

"But he told the truth, didn't he?"

"Yes. But sometimes it's better to keep the truth to oneself."

Cele and her son fell into silence. Only the ticking of the clock broke the stillness. Outside, the faraway bark of a dog echoed. In a few hours, Sebastián and Ignacio would be leaving their family and home; in the meantime, mother and son were aware of time slipping away yet powerless to stop it. Then the clock chimed; it was nearly daybreak, the darkest hour of the night. The time had come to leave.

When silence took over, Dolores slithered out from her hiding place to go to her bed and sleep. She had wanted to know everything, hear everything, and now she was convinced that her mother had not broken their vow. Later on, asleep in her bed, noises coming from the rear corral awoke her, and she went to the window where she watched Sebastián and her father say goodbye to Cele.

Although just a foggy memory, years later, she still remembered the sadness she felt at that moment; it was the hurt of separation she had never experienced before. She made out her father as he mounted his mule and then watched Sebastián kneel at Cele's feet for her blessing.

In that hour of darkness, Dolores saw her mother's raised arm and outstretched fingers as she traced the sign of the cross on her brother's forehead, something Cele always did whenever her children were to be separated from her.

Dolores stood on tiptoes, stretching her neck to keep sight of them for as long as she could, but her father and brother soon disappeared into the gloom. She stared into that emptiness, hoping to make out at least a part of them, but there was nothing, they became blurred silhouettes swallowed by the mist, leaving behind only the sound of clopping hooves on cobblestones. Her brother and father began the trek north at daybreak on a dreary day in 1919.

CHAPTER SIX

The Fever

SOMETIME DURING that bleak year, a mysterious disease made its way into Dolores's town when a stranger strolled into the crowded outdoor market. He quietly looked around, sometimes picking up an apple or an orange, turning it over carefully, yet not buying it. He simply gazed at the merchant lady, smiled, and moved on to the next stand to again scrutinize its vegetables and fruits. After a while, he paused to chat with one or two people, then he moved on but stopped when a sudden sneezing attack assaulted him. Those people close by thought his wheezing was amusing, so they laughed out loud but then politely wished him a friendly *salud*. The stranger moved on and disappeared into the crowd, still sneezing and coughing.

The next day, early Mass had to be postponed to a later time because, as the notice explained, Father Gabriel was dealing with a bad cold and slight fever. Father Rufino would be available for a later Mass. Please return, said the note. However, when the devout congregation returned, yet another notice was posted saying that Father Gabriel's condition had taken a serious turn. Please pray for him, and people were asked to offer their Mass for his recovery.

This is the way the dread pandemic flu began, sweeping its way from unknown parts of the United States, from there to that little town in Mexico and farther south until it wrapped its fearful arms around the entire world. In that small town from which Ignacio and Sebastián Gómez had just begun their trek north, people died quick painful deaths. When stricken, a person healthy in the morning was dead by evening. First came the coughing and sneezing and then the tightness in the throat, followed by a relentless fever. Soon after came the vomit, black, gummy, and then death. This sickness lasted no more than a few hours.

Panic followed the deadly illness; no one could understand what was happening nor how to protect themselves.

Don't leave your house! Keep vinegar close by to smear on your nostrils! Burn marijuana! Its smoke cleanses the air. Wear a mask if you leave your home! Pray to the Virgin Mary!

Warnings raged, passing from house to house. Stores, schools, and markets shut down, even the church shut its heavy portals. No one dared leave the protection of their home, but still, the creeping death made its way through cracks and open windows killing everyone in its path. People tried to keep up their traditions of vigils and funerals and prayers but quickly saw that this only made it worse; more people died when they came close to one another, so they isolated. The dead were quickly buried without ceremony, and when the coffin maker ran out of coffins, bodies were wrapped in shrouds and put that way into the earth.

The Spanish Flu had made its way into the Gómez family, but none perished; they escaped, not knowing how or why. Ignacio and Sebastián also faced the menace up north, and they, too, lived through the panic.

CHAPTER SEVEN

Nearing Constantinople

FAR FROM mexico, the Great War and then the dreaded flu uprooted people and shattered homes and families, leaving thousands of displaced people in search of shelter and safety. Those fugitives, migrants, and exiles who had not perished because of starvation or the sickness kept on the move, making their way from Lebanon through Syria and into Turkey.

Embedded in that surge, the old woman and the boy, raggedy and starving, pushed their way toward a sanctuary she said awaited them in Constantinople. Walking alongside Zepyur and David were the decent and the innocent, but also among them were frauds and schemers, thieves and pickpockets, misfits that lived on whatever could be snatched, maybe a worthless bauble, or even a stale crust of bread.

Sometimes they moved in the middle of a cluster of three or four nameless strangers. At other times, they melted into a faceless throng, without knowing anyone, or where they came from; it meant nothing after all. What mattered was that they were bound together by suffering, pain, hunger, cold, alienation, and a desperate drive for survival.

Villages melted into towns: Tartus, Latakia, Idleb, and even Aleppo. The old woman and the boy ate what others shared with them. Other times, they begged for food, but sometimes David, forced to become a thief, ran off with a loaf of bread, or even a salted fish. But not always, because there were times when he did small things in exchange for a coin to purchase something to eat. Zepyur, too, did her part by reading the palm of a merchant or soldier in exchange for a few coins, or by simply sitting by the roadside where a kind-hearted sojourner took pity on her.

As they trekked toward Constantinople, the days grew long, hot, and tedious; so Zepyur told stories to pass time. She told of legends and fables and histories, but the one that most entranced David was the one she related about her mother and father's journey to Córdoba when she was still a girl.

"Where is that city?"

David asked because he had never heard of such a place.

"Córdoba is in Spain. It's where you will guide me in time, so listen to what I'm about to tell because it will prepare you."

He was intrigued to know he was to be her guide to a city in a country he had never heard of, so he listened.

"I was a girl about your age when my mother and father's roaming took us to the uppermost regions of Africa to a city named Maruecos, or as other people say, Marrakesh. From there, we went on to Tangiers and to the edge of the ocean where we put our caravan on a barge that ferried us onto the shores of Spain. On that trip, we drifted by a huge rock called Gibraltar before touching land in Algeciras, and from there, we made our way to the great city once known as the Caliphate of Córdoba."

David listened to Zepyur's words because they transported him to distant lands and time, to desert cities and fortresses. His eyes longed to see what she had seen. He wanted to smell the fragrances of the marketplaces and hear the sounds she had experienced while in the heart of kasbahs and mysterious streets.

"Do you think I'll ever see such a city?"

"Yes! That will be the end of our journey."

When she saw his mouth open to ask more about what she had just said, she held a bony finger to her lips to let David know that he should listen and not ask questions.

"Córdoba is the city where the magnificent Mezquita is to be found, the mosque of a thousand pillars, the most exquisite in the world of Islam. There's a Christian chapel now located in that temple's center, a place of worship erected for the great Queen Isabel."

The boy was anxious to ask questions. What was a chapel? Who was the great Queen Isabel? But he knew by then that once Zepyur had begun a story, interruptions were not allowed, so he listened.

"My mother, father, and I made our way through the city's narrow, winding streets until we reached a tiny plaza in the Jewish Quarter, very close to *la Mezquita.* It was there that we encountered a crowd witnessing a chess game that had been going on for days."

This time, he could not hold back.

"What sort of game is chess?"

"It's a contest of wit, cunning, and style, but mostly strategy. It's played by two illustrious people, but because it's a challenge to any human being's intelligence, not everyone is disposed to engage in such a match. As for those who witness the contest, complete silence is mandatory since the contestants must concentrate without distraction. It was into that quiet that my parents and I entered. It was an unforgettable experience."

Zepyur then fell silent, as if her memory had transported her to that fabled city of ancient pathways and the many-pillared mosque, but because David was anxious to hear more about the game, he broke into her musings.

"Tell more of the game."

"I know little about it other than that it's conducted on a board set up on a table, and that it has two contestants. The one I witnessed was being played by a scholarly Jew named Ben Ezra and an equally accomplished and wise Muslim named Al Mansur."

"Who told you their names?"

"I don't know."

"Yet you remember those names after so many years?"

"I cannot explain how it is that I remember after so long. I just do."

"Do you remember the rules of the game?"

"Only vague words such as king, queen, knight, and pawn, expressions that describe the pieces used in the contest. And then there is checkmate, or a word that sounds like it, a most important move of the game because it tells that one of the players has been blocked, and that he cannot move. That's what I think it means. When this happens, the end of the match is at hand, a winner is soon to emerge if his defense continues cunningly."

Zepyur wrinkled her brow, trying to recall more but then shook her head.

"Well, that's all I can remember about the game itself. Now I'll return to my memory of the match that was happening when my mother, father, and I joined the crowd. I was intent on watching and listening, so I soon overheard whispering that the contest had been going on for hours, and that the only interruption had taken place for the players to refresh themselves. Can you imagine such a thing, young David?"

"No, I cannot. Did you stay to the end?"

"I did, but only because by the time we joined the contest it was already at the defense stage."

"Zepyur, who won the match?"

"Patience! I'm getting to that part. The end could easily have gone one way or the other, but I sensed that the Muslim had more backers in the crowd than did the Jew. I felt tension in the crowd, even a hidden anger, probably because people were fatigued from the strain of waiting for so long. Also, chess is a game of wager, and certainly, many of those people had placed bets, no doubt hefty ones, so you can imagine there was an investment on the part of many of those men. I think having to keep silent also added to the tension. Yes, there was a feeling of strong emotions that hung over the crowd like a gloomy cloud."

"Who won?"

"When I heard the word 'Checkmate!,' I stretched my neck to see from behind that wall of shoulders and turbaned heads, and I realized the words had come from the Muslim. He had outwitted the Jew. He was the winner!"

"And then?"

"At first there was quiet, but then the spell was suddenly shattered by deep grunt-like sounds filled with words I did not understand, but that I supposed meant *cheater, thief, Muslim ferret*! Perhaps the meaning of those words was even worse, the thing is that turbulence broke out. There was shoving, scuffling, and flinging fists among those people that had stood in friendly silence just minutes before. This was followed by harsher insulting words, and I could tell those men were cursing one another. At one point, I looked toward the atrium of la Mezquita searching for a way out but saw only a blur of robes and turbans and beards, all in a flurry of angry conflict.

"Frightened, I looked for my mother and father who were crouching a few steps away from me. As I lunged toward them through that mob, I caught the glint of a drawn curved dagger. I didn't have time to close my eyes, so I saw when that blade plunged into my mother's breast."

Alarmed, David stammered, "Why would anyone want to harm your mother?"

David was shocked. He struggled to understand why such a terrible act could follow what was supposed to be a game, why an innocent woman was attacked. On the other hand, had he not witnessed his own mother's murder on the death march? Without a word, David got closer to Zepyur, yearning to put his head on her shoulder just to let her know that he felt her grief.

"I have never found the explanation for that terrible act except that it was the deed of an evil person who perhaps mistakenly thought she was a Muslim woman, or perhaps a Jewish one. Who knows what is in the heart of such a wicked person? I don't know. What I do know is that although the knife struck close to her heart, it gave her enough time to speak a few last words.

"'Take me into the chapel to look at its pillars and arches before I die. Lay me on its altar.'

"That's what she said. And although it was difficult, Father and I carried her through the labyrinth of pillars. I still remember the scraping of our footsteps on the stone floor as well as the echo of our breathing as we did it. It's all still so vivid! We struggled, but we finally reached the altar where we laid her. It was there, in our arms, that my mother breathed her last sigh and where we washed her face with our tears."

David was struck silent, but then, he finally murmured, "I'm sorry, Old One. It hurts so much to lose one's mother. I know."

"David, don't feel that way. My mother went to heaven the way she wanted, from the place she desired most. Do you remember I told you that she was of the Egyptian Coptic people? They are Christians, and to die in such a cradle of worship has no parallel in their way of thinking."

"Where did you bury her body?"

"No, it didn't happen that way. Father and I took her body to the outskirts of Córdoba to an isolated place where he built a pyre with wood we gathered, and there we placed the body and set it on fire. She was frail and her remains were consumed quickly. I'm certain I saw her spirit ascend to paradise."

"You saw her spirit? What did it look like?"

Zepyur turned to look at David with an intense gaze. She kept quiet and did not answer his question. Puzzled, he thought it best to move on to another of the many questions swirling in his head.

"What did you do with her ashes?"

"Father put most of them into an urn, and the rest of them he packed into a small jar for me to keep. Look! I have it here in my satchel! I've carried her ashes with me these many years as I've wandered."

"But what about the man who killed your mother?"

"What about him?"

"Was he caught?"

"Not that I know."

"Do you regret the man wasn't punished?"

"No, David. My mother was in paradise, no longer suffering. What would we gain by capturing and punishing anyone?"

"I don't know. Perhaps you and your father would have gotten some satisfaction."

"Satisfaction disappears and leaves nothing but a bitter taste in one's mouth."

David kept quiet when Zepyur finished speaking. He was conflicted by thoughts and questions. He longed to have been her companion at a time when they would have been the same age, when they would have seen the world in the same way. He wished he had been by her side as she carried her mother into the mysterious chapel, and that he could have journeyed from one country to the other by her side. But now it was too late; she was too old, and he, too young.

And then, as if reading her companion's thoughts, Zepyur said, "It's not too late, young David. We still have time to see many places and get to know different people. After all, you're my guide, aren't you? Will you not allow me to take your shoulder as we make our way to Córdoba?"

"La Mezquita?"

"Yes! As I've already told you, that city will mark the end of our journey. It's where I will die, and where you will see that my remains are consumed by fire."

"Old Woman, will you die of the fever that has taken so many?"

"No, David. It will not be of the fever, nor will you perish because of it, but you will leave it behind after you scatter my ashes to the winds that sweep across the ocean from Africa."

With nothing more to say, Zepyur clasped her hand on David's shoulder. She was ready to go on with their pilgrimage destined to take them on stony pathways and roads leading to Constantinople and then to Córdoba. Their first year ended.

CHAPTER EIGHT

Out of Mexico

THE YEAR ended for Dolores and her family still terrorized by the relentless fever that swept through their town, forcing them into an isolation made even worse because they had yet not heard from Ignacio or Sebastián. Long days turned into longer months until, at last, word came; it was time. Although it was what Cele and her children were waiting for, they felt afraid. At first they were filled with excitement, but then it turned to anxiety. The only thing that calmed them was that other families were doing the same thing and taking the same risks. Dolores and her family were among the late-starters, making them feel a little better to think that maybe they would meet friends over there on the other side.

Hardly stopping to eat or sleep, putting aside the precautions she had taken because of the epidemic, Cele sold their house and other things and had her children pack only what they could carry on the train headed for Nogales, a city far to the north.

"Your father and brother will meet us there."

They packed, but none of them imagined that what lay ahead would be so brutal. Cele and her children did not have an inkling of the unknown that waited for them, beginning with days on a crowded second-class train with bare wooden benches, small windows, some that opened, others that were stuck, trapping them in stifling desert heat.

Once the day came to leave, the family faced the train so dismayed they did not know what to do, but Cele was quick to push them on board before they knew what was happening. Once on board, Dolores was first to claim a place by a window where she intended to stay for the rest of the journey. After her, the rest filed in to find a place where they waited quiet and afraid.

They had barely settled when the train suddenly lurched forward with a jerk that caught the packed-in passengers by surprise. Bundles and packets flew off the overhead shelves, landing here and there on the aisle, on laps, and even on startled heads. Arms and legs jerked, trying to keep steady; those who had never been on a train fought off panic, wide-eyed and pale. Others, knowing what was happening, regained their balance, and then after the commotion was over, they chuckled, just a little embarrassed by their clumsiness.

During that rough departure, Dolores sat taking it all in, staring at the ragtag collection of passengers. Some wore homemade masks; others tried to protect themselves by holding a handkerchief or the edge of a shawl to cover their nose. Most were peasants, displaced or chased off confiscated land; others shut out of their huts, or maybe marauding bandits and renegades had trampled their maize or bean patches, leaving them to starve. They were homeless people with terrified children that clung to a hand or shirttail, people who carried what they owned pasted on their backs, or stuffed into a gunnysack.

"Mama." Dolores looked over at Cele. "Who are these people?"

"People like us, Dolores." Cele, getting more tired by the minute, glared at the girl. "Now, sit back and try to sleep."

But Dolores was not sleepy; instead, she went on staring at those people. She looked at the men's tattered, sweat-soaked straw sombreros, their soiled homespun shirts and baggy pants, as well as the women's threadbare faded dresses and shawls. Had she been older, she would have sensed that although expressionless, behind those craggy brown faces were hearts broken by loss and anxiety.

Peasant farm workers were the majority of passengers that had clawed their way aboard the train heading north. But there were others, a handful of city people who had their own reasons for fleeing. Anyone could recognize them by the way they sat, stiff and aloof on those uncomfortable wooden benches, trying to keep up just the right appearance, one that said "I belong to a better class than you." It was an attitude that desperately tried to cover up the obvious: that they had barely scraped up enough money to buy a second-class ticket to nowhere, just like the pack of peasants surrounding them.

The men of that class were dressed in faded dark blue or gray serge ill-fitting suits, frayed shirt collars kept in place by a washed out tie, maybe even a tie clasp, and because it was just the beginning of the trip, their worn-out two-toned shoes were polished. Once-fashionable straw hats, of course, topped the outfit.

Their women were dressed in what must have been their Sunday outfit, along with faded gloves, matching purse, and a hat topped by a droopy feather, or maybe tiny artificial flowers. Those women sat with eyes modestly cast down, backs held rigid by a corset, and knees tightly clasped together.

It was obvious that none of those city folks had prepared for the hardships of riding in a second-class coach packed with nervous, coarse passengers that had scrambled for a place. Those city passengers had not thought that soon their clothes would hang on them like rags, and that their sweat would stink just as much as that of their peasant companions.

But there was yet another cluster of travelers on board, those who were neither city people nor field workers. They were the small-town dwellers—owners of the local grocery store, the tobacco shop, the town distillery, or even the herb and medicinal store. It was to this group that Cele Gómez and her children belonged, and although they felt different, there was a thread that tied them to the rest of the passengers. They, too, felt the anxiety of not knowing what was waiting for them at the end of their journey.

Dolores finally slumped back in her seat and closed her eyes while images floated under her eyelids: field workers, men in suits, women with children, suitcases, boxes, masks, and the sour smell of people shoved one against the other. It was only then that she drifted off to sleep lulled by the sway and pull of the train's rhythm, and her last thought was, *Dios mío, we are all going to die of the epidemic.*

CHAPTER NINE

Constantinople

DAVID HAD never seen such a wondrous sight! In the distance, he saw turrets, domes, spires, and mosques; gold, silver, lavender, and blue tiles reflected the sun's light creating a vision too splendid for him to take in. In the midst of a fast-moving current of wanderers and refugees, Zepyur and David stood at the entrance of the Galata Bridge with Asia at their backs and Europe in front of them.

Although only months had passed, he was almost a man, young and filled with powerful urges and thoughts. As he stood gazing at that vast panorama, a violent mix of emotions gripped him: fascination brought on by the beauty of that city mixed in with a profound sadness knowing that behind lay his plundered homeland, as well as the scattered remains of his family.

"Come, David!" called out Zepyur, and he followed as they began the trek from one side of the world into the other.

David sensed he was on the edge of an ancient world, and when he took his first footstep onto the bridge, he knew it was the pathway to the rest of his life.

"What's on the other side, Old One?"

"It is the city of seven hills where we will find the shrine of Holy Wisdom, as well as the mosque of Sultan Ahmed."

"How will we do it? We don't have money. We don't even know where to sleep tonight."

"It will become evident."

"When?"

"Soon."

"And what about those officials who ask for papers? We've been lucky so far when they've just pushed us forward with the rest of the wanderers."

"As they will do so from now on. No one will take notice of us, David, there are too many of us, and those officials only want to get rid of us. They will drive us out of their way as soon as they can."

But David was unconvinced, and after a minute, he blurted out, "Are you sure?"

"I'm sure. Now let us move toward the center of the old city where we will find shelter and food. Have faith, David, have faith."

It didn't take long before they were among a mass of merchants and buyers mixed in with pickpockets, beggars, camel drivers, and sheepherders—people from everywhere. David was transfixed, hemmed in by hawkers screaming out their wares, creating a babble of languages and dialects. On one side, he saw mounds of spices, roots, and herbs. Zepyur stopped to name some of them.

"Look, David! Saffron and basil, right there. See? There you have mint and oregano and even aniseed to cure ailments. And in those large bowls you see in that stall are the favorites of so many countries: turmeric, cinnamon, cumin, and nutmeg."

Near him were gold and silver ornaments, exquisitely worked jewelry, and over there was clothing of luxurious materials, as well as coarse ware for shepherds, camel drivers, and tavern keepers.

"Come, worthy customer!" one merchant shouted. "Come and sample this perfume that has traveled all the way from a secret Arabian seraglio. Come and see how the fragrance will enhance your beloved's delicate throat!"

"No! Do not heed that lying voice," shouted his competitor. "Look, instead, at this veil that has truly crossed the vast desert over the Silk Road just to recline on her fair shoulders!"

High-pitched shouting, wailing, and cursing cut through and around the countless stalls, creating a powerful din that seduced the multitude of travelers crowded onto the ancient cobblestones of that bazaar. And in the middle of the din and commotion, David pushed his way forward, all the time conscious of Zepyur's hand clasped on his shoulder. When he felt that she had paused, he turned to look; when she spoke, her voice was drowned out by the noise, so he had to bend down to put his ear close to her lips.

"Look over there, David." She pointed a bony finger at a man seated at a table, evidently concentrating on something he was writing. "Over there! That's the man we must speak to. He will be the one to help us."

David caught a glimpse of a man with a long gray beard; with a striped shawl covering his head, he was hunched over the document he was writing. *Maybe he's blind*, thought David.

Without hesitating, David cut a path toward the man surrounded by piles of parchments nearly covering the floor of his stall, along with a table loaded with more papers and pots of ink, each one with a quill. When Zepyur and David reached the man's table, he looked up at them with blinking gray eyes; it took him a while to focus.

"Good evening, Venerable Scribe." Zepyur was the first to speak.

"Good day to you, Honored Lady." His voice was warm and sonorous. He made an attempt to get to his feet but then had to fall back onto his chair. "Forgive me for not rising. My legs no longer support me. In what way may I be of service to you and your grandson?"

David's head snapped to look at Zepyur to hear what she would answer. He saw, however, that she made no attempt to correct the mistake; instead, she cleared her throat and smacked her wrinkled lips.

"Venerable Scribe, we're travelers from far, and we're hungry and thirsty." She turned to the boy, still with her hand on his shoulder. "David is a sturdy boy, as you can see, and he can be your helper in whatever manner you ask, in return for a jug of water, a loaf of bread, and possibly a corner in which we may sleep for the night."

The man, his brow wrinkled in thought, leaned back in the chair. "Hmm!" That was the only sound he let out as he gazed at David and Zepyur while he ran his fingers up and down his thick beard. "Hmm!"

He again let out the same sound, a mix of a sigh and a groan. Then he focused his gaze on David, "Tell me, young master, are you intelligent?"

Although taken by surprise, David answered, "Yes, Maestro! As intelligent as God has ordained."

Obviously impressed with David's answer, the scribe went on to ask more questions. "I see you speak a form of Turkish. Where are you from?"

"From Old Armenia, Maestro."

"And what brings you so far away from your homeland?"

"The Turks killed my family, stole our land, and condemned me to an orphanage. But when those same Turks were dispersed, I escaped. The Old One standing here by my side, Zepyur, saved me, and so here I am."

"She is not your grandmother?"

"No, Maestro."

"Hmm!" Again the same half sigh, half groan slipped out of the scribe's mouth. He turned his gaze to Zepyur, who stood patiently listening to his questions.

"Venerable Lady, I have chores the boy can do right away so that you may have your water, food, and a place to sleep. I will think more as to what he can do for me after today. The man turned to the boy. "What is your name?"

"David Katagian, Maestro. And this is my guide, Zepyur. She has no family name."

For the first time, the scribe smiled. "I am known as Abenray, a public writer of letters and documents. Most important, I am a Sephardic Jew, born in Baku in what was Russia of the Czars. I have much to teach you, David Katagian. That is, if you are, indeed, intelligent."

On that day, David became the Scribe's apprentice in charge of keeping order to the countless bundles of documents, as well as the library kept in the Scribe's residence. There were many other chores, even minor ones, such as seeing to it that inkpots were filled and quills sharpened, ready for use, and David did them all.

CHAPTER TEN

From Mexico to el Norte

AS THE train picked up speed, its loud clanking drowned out the passengers' chitchat so they stopped talking and dozed; soon heads wobbled comically, making the kids giggle. Dolores Gómez was one of them, but she was soon distracted by the passing views. First it was the town's outskirts, and then buildings and outhouses faded until it was open space. After a full day's travel, the land shifted from rolling hills to craggy cliffs until it became warmer and sticky. From time to time, when her eyes began to hurt, Dolores looked away from the window to gaze at her family.

They filled two face-to-face benches where her mother and Pilar held aisle seats. *Like two guards*, thought Dolores. Altagracia snuggled onto Cele's side where she would stay for the rest of the journey, even after stops and trips to the toilet. Esperanza and Héctor, trying to look cocky and independent, sat facing each other, sometimes making faces or trading signs with their hands or pointing to this or that funny-looking passenger.

Esperanza and Héctor were the clowns of the family, and Dolores was the one who watched but lost track of time to the point that she did not know how many days passed while they were on that train.

What she disliked most were the nights because they had to sleep on the hard floor of the coach on coats and bundles her mother and Pilar put down for them. When their packed food ran out, Cele and Héctor got off the train at stops to buy tortillas and other things to eat. All of this, Dolores found boring and dull.

"Guaymas! Guaymas!"

With husky shouts, the porter woke up the passengers early one day, announcing the city with a strange name.

"Mama, where are we?"

"I don't know, Dolores. It's far north, and close to where your father and brother are waiting for us."

Mumbling, groaning, and stretching people craned their necks to peer through grimy windows to catch a glimpse of the last city on the coast; soon, the train would head eastward into the desert, and then northward on to Nogales on the Mexican side of the border.

"Señor, are we going to spend some time here?"

"No, señora. We've lost too much time as it is. The train is stopping just long enough to load water for the engine, and then forward we go. So please don't even think of getting off."

He was right. After much running around and shouting on the ground, rail workers moved out of the way, and the train again lurched forward with a violent jerk, picking up speed faster than at other departures. People looked at one another, sensing something different; nervousness spread from the front of the coach to its rear.

"I don't like this!"

"What do you mean?"

"Well, there are bandits and other riffraff on the roads, you know. No! I don't like it that we aren't taking time in Guaymas. The porter could have at least told us the reason."

Two people upfront didn't even try to keep their fears to themselves, most everyone overheard them, and Dolores caught the look between Pilar and her mother. It was just a glance, but it shared some kind of tension.

"Mama, what's going to happen?"

"Nothing, Dolores. Try to nap a little bit more."

Dolores was about to pull her mother's sleeve when the train suddenly slammed on the breaks, skidding until it came to a screeching halt, again sending passengers, bundles, and other things flying. The rocking and shaking caused anger in some of the passengers, in others, fear.

"Bandits! Do you think we're going to be robbed?"

"No! Calm down! There's probably something wrong with the engine."

"You're wrong! I think it's something worse than engine problems. We're going to be robbed, I tell you!"

Again the edgy passengers spat out their unease, and a low hum of mumbling and whispering swept the coach. People felt that there was reason for nervousness since the Revolution wasn't really over; marauding gangs of misfits were still everywhere on the highways, and even the railways.

"Mama, look!"

Dolores, nose pressed against the window, caught sight of a gang of riders, nearly lost in billows of whirling dust, their horses moving closer to the coach. Some, more in the distance, were galloping toward the train, but others were already so close their riders were clinging to the side of the coach. She tried to count them.

"Five! Ten! Thirteen! Mama, there's so many of them! I think there's more than twenty!"

Dolores's voice was the alarm that sent most of the passengers scrambling to her side of the coach, all of them crowding in on top of one another, elbowing and pushing, trying to catch a glimpse of what the girl was yelling about. By then, the passengers were shouting frantically, but the racket suddenly stopped when three armed men burst into the coach. Two were dressed like revolutionaries: a sombrero nearly covering their faces, the baggy homespun ragged white pants and shirt, the worn-out huaraches. The third man looked like a city dweller, as if he had just left his desk at a library, or maybe a bank. He wore a dark-blue pinstriped serge suit. His shirt was clean; its starched collar just beginning to show a sweaty stain. The only thing that made him one with his comrades was the heavy bandoleer crisscrossing his chest, and the Winchester rifle he gripped.

The passengers froze, eyes locked on the intruders while a scary silence filled the coach's dusty air. What felt like an unending moment crept by until one of the assailants growled, "Viva Cristo Rey!" The man paused, showing he expected something, maybe a reply, but there was nothing. After a moment, he repeated, "Viva Cristo Rey!"

This time, someone had the nerve to shout out in response, "Viva!"

Dolores, hiding behind her mother, peered out to see what was happening, but all she saw were the backs of men and women who stood frozen. But nothing was happening, neither intruders nor passengers moved; they glared at one another until the man who had shouted out turned his back and left the coach. His henchmen followed him. Again, people rushed to the windows to see what was happening, confused because they saw the raiders gallop away with the same urgency as when they had ambushed the train. Now the grumbling and questioning started.

"What's going on?"

"What does this mean?"

"What did those no-goods want?"

"Quick! Look around! Are all the women here?"

Cele jumped to make sure her daughters were still with her, as did everyone else; relief came over everyone when no one was missing. There were loud sighs, nervous coughing here and there; some passengers scratched their heads, trying to make sense of what had happened, and others chuckled nervously, thinking maybe they had overreacted, nearly fallen to pieces just because of three ragged nobodies. Word went from passenger to passenger:

"Those losers were probably trying to recruit people to join their ranks. That's all! Where's the porter when we need him?"

The only one that detected a difference was Dolores who had been crouching behind her mother; it was from there that she saw a young man quietly climb into the coach while the big scare was going on, when all eyes were on the intruders up front. She saw him slither in through the rear door and slip into an empty space crunched into the rear corner. Dolores had seen him do that, and so had Esperanza, but both kept it to themselves.

From there, the train cranked up its engine and sped headlong into the desert, hardly stopping at stations, sometimes pausing in the middle of nowhere to load up on water and coal. The heat grew more intense with each hour, barely cooling off even after the sun dipped behind the horizon, a mysterious moment when the tall saguaro cactuses cast shadows that looked like giants with uplifted arms.

Dolores loved the night when the travelers slept, when the whirr and clanging of the train mellowed to a soft lulling hum. She forced herself to stay awake just to gaze at the passing darkness with its starry shroud high above. She imagined those stars were eyes, maybe of angels, or maybe the eyes of people who had died but still watched. Although it was so hot, even during those dark hours, Dolores loved it because they were hours that belonged to her.

During the daylight hours, she noticed how Esperanza and the young straggler looked at each other, not once or twice, but many times, and their gazes were filled with words, as if they knew each other. Once, during the warmest time of the day, when just about everybody was dozing, Dolores happened to open her eyes in time to see her sister sitting with the stranger in his corner, very close, holding hands and whispering. Dolores's head snapped over to look up at her mother to see if she was looking, but Cele was dozing too. When Dolores turned to take another look, Esperanza was not there anymore; only the young man sat looking out the window, and Esperanza was back at her place pretending to nap.

One of those nights, Dolores was awake, enjoying the starry sky until she sensed someone moving in the gloom. She sat up to see what was happening, and she made out Esperanza creeping toward the stranger where she finally slipped in to sit close to him. Intrigued, Dolores decided to watch no matter how many hours it took. Sleep, however, overcame her; and it took the porter's loud voice early next morning to wake her up.

"Señores, señoras, start to get ready! Nogales is less than one hour away, and everyone has to be ready to leave this train immediately. No time to lose! Get ready! Make sure you have all your things! Make sure the children will be ready!"

The porter's voice was so loud it snapped everyone awake and into action. Some people, eyes half closed, jumped up to gather belongings from the upper racks; others dragged valises and parcels from under their seats. Most of the women's hands flew up to pat down uncombed hair and to smooth tired faces. Cele got to her feet, wobbly and stiff from so many hours of sitting, but she was herself soon.

"Children, gather your bags and other things. Don't forget anything! Pilar, help me with these bundles! Héctor and Dolores stay close to me no matter how many people we find at the station, and Altagracia, hold on to Esperanza's hand. Don't let go!"

Cele turned to her brood as she parceled out what to do, so when she uttered Esperanza's name, she looked around for her, but she was not in her usual place.

"Esperanza?"

Cele swiveled in every direction, as did the rest of her family, looking up and down the aisle, stretching, trying to look around and behind passengers already on their feet. The sway of the train made her cling to the back of the bench to keep from falling.

"Esperanza!"

Each time she repeated her daughter's name, Cele's voice became louder, and then even shrill. Soon other passengers helped by calling out the young woman's name, but Esperanza was nowhere to be seen. Over the din and swaying of the train, Cele's voice became filled with panic, alarming everyone. One of the men ran to the next coach and returned with the porter.

"Señora, explain what's happened to this official."

"How can I explain? I don't know what happened, or when, but my daughter is missing. Please help me! Stop the train! We must go back!"

The flustered official tried to help the distressed woman. "Señora, we can't stop the train, much less go back. The only thing we can do is look for her in the other coaches. I'm sure she just wandered off to look around, or maybe make a friend. That's probably the explanation."

The man turned to the other passengers crowding around, alarm and curiosity stamped on their faces.

"Señora, please come with me so we can find your daughter. If she's on the train, then we will certainly find her."

Cele was quick to answer, "*If*? What do you mean *If*? Could she have fallen off? What, in the name of God, could have happened to her?"

"Señora, please! Remember, we had two stops during the night. The last was four hours ago. She could have gotten off at either stop."

Cele and Pilar's face became wooden, and the children looked at one another, distressed to think their sister was somewhere back there, miles away, alone, and probably crying.

"There are three coaches connected to this one on the rear, and four in front. Señora, you and your son"—the porter pointed at Héctor—"check the rear cars, and you, señorita," he pointed at Pilar, "come with me to search the others. When you're finished, return here, and your daughter and I will also return when we finish searching. Don't be afraid! We'll find your daughter. Again, what's her name?"

"Esperanza!"

Five voices answered the official at once. Cele's family was now one, pulled together by alarm.

"Mama, let me come with you. Please!"

"No, Dolores. You have to stay here with Altagracia. If Esperanza comes, tell her to wait for us, and don't move."

With Héctor's hand clutched in hers, Cele lunged toward the rear door of the coach, yelling out as she made her way down the aisle of the first car and then the next one.

"Esperanza! Esperanza! Has anyone seen my daughter? She's fifteen years old, has long dark hair, and she's wearing a blue dress."

"Mama she's wearing a brown dress!" Héctor tugged at Cele's hand, but she did not pay attention to him. She kept on yelling as they cut their way through another rear door into the next coach, but it was not until they reached the last one that several passengers blocked Cele's way.

"Señora, please stop for a moment!"

A middle-aged man, dressed in a dusty suit and tie, grasped her arm. Cele's heart was racing with anxiety and fear, so she stopped but answered in a barely audible voice.

"What do you want? Let us through!"

"Señora, my son, too, is missing. I think he got off during the night at one of the stops, and I suspect he was with someone. Maybe it was your daughter."

Stunned, Cele squinted at the man trying to take in what he was saying. Questions and doubts zigzagged through her mind until she finally understood what he was saying.

"Why would my daughter follow a stranger off the train without telling me? Who is your son anyway? What a foolish thing for you to think. My daughter is a good girl! Who do you think you are?"

Cele's rage made her blurt out disconnected, unreasonable words, but the man stood quietly, allowing her to jabber.

"My son's name is Regino Nájera, and he, too, is a good boy." The man spoke slowly; his voice was filled with hurt yet calm. "But I regret to say that he's a follower of the Cristeros, and maybe your daughter is part of that band."

Cele's body stiffened. Something in the man's words, in the way he spoke deeply alarmed her because they rang true, and they made her think.

Los Cristeros! That band of fanatics! Aren't they the ones who forced their way onto our coach? Maybe some invaded the other coaches at the same time. Did Esperanza strike up a friendship with one of them behind my back? Did I miss something my daughter was doing with this man's son? Was she dragged away, or did she go willingly?

"What can I do?" Cele's voice was filled with tears even though her eyes were dry.

"Nothing. For my part, all I can do is return to where my son might have left this train, but I have to wait until we arrive at Nogales. I'll have to get the name of the stops the train made last night and then return to search for him. I'm sorry, señora."

As the man spoke, Cele understood what had happened. She did not need more explanations; neither did she have to investigate. Esperanza had been seduced by the sickening piety of the Cristero message. Of all her children, Esperanza was the most inclined to devotion; she had been that way since she was little often saying she wanted to become a nun. It would have been easy for those fanatics to persuade her.

"I'm grateful, señor. Please forgive my bad manner. Come, Héctor!"

Cele took her son's hand and pulled him toward their coach. People looked at her with pity, yet they knew that what had happened to her and her daughter was not new. The Cristero movement was just beginning, but already, the zealots among them were asserting themselves in whatever way they could.

That's what the train invasion was all about. It was to abduct followers. There are many girls like Esperanza Gómez, as well as young dreamers like Regino Nájera. This is nothing but the beginning of a new wave of suffering, and we have nothing to do but brace ourselves. A shame!

This is what the passengers thought. Some came out with it, but others kept it to themselves.

CHAPTER ELEVEN

The Apprentice

DAVID WORKED hard, and in exchange, he learned much from his mentor. For instance, Master Abenray taught David serious reading as well as calligraphy, and he was introduced to languages spoken in Constantinople. The boy was quick, and he picked up first on scattered words; after that, he began to lace together sentences, and soon, he was able to converse, even if it was in a mix of Arabic, Hebrew, Greek, and even bits of Sephardic Spanish. The Scribe's clients often burst out laughing at his gibberish, but David did not mind. On the contrary, he laughed along, even slapping his thigh to show that he was aware of his foolishness. And soon, David's good nature was noticed, and he was liked by all those patrons.

He and Zepyur resided with Abenray for years as the boy grew under his master teacher's guidance. As for Zepyur, she became a part of that tiny family bringing it warmth, heart, and words of wisdom for her young companion. All along she bided her time until the day when she and David saved enough coin to move on to Córdoba.

During those years, she and David scoured Constantinople's unknown parts. The dark, smoky taverns and inns were especially alluring to him, as was the loud laughter and music that spilled out onto the street through their dim doors. Each time he passed such a

Dreamers

place, he yearned to find out what the mariners and merchants found so enjoyable. *Was it those women with painted faces and lifted breasts?* He wondered. Even when working by Master Abenray's side, these thoughts intrigued David, and many times, images of those women recurred no matter how much he tried to get rid of them. Despite his struggle, the urge to get close to at least one of those mysterious women got stronger each day.

It happened one day when he was about to place a pile of papers on a shelf when the image of one of those women, her breasts nearly exposed, came to him so vividly he stood captivated, the stack teetering in his hands.

"David."

The teacher's unexpected voice startled him, and the wobbly pile fell and scattered over the floor. David lunged, trying to retrieve the mess, thinking that, for sure, Abenray was about to scold him.

"You have been a good disciple, David Katagian."

"Thank you, Maestro." David gratefully murmured, "You have been a good teacher."

"How old are you now?"

"I'm seventeen."

"Hmm!"

David stopped what he was doing to gaze at his mentor. He wondered what the scribe was thinking.

"You've been faithful to the gifts God has given you. You've learned."

"Thank you, Maestro."

Then the old Jew slipped into a deep silence, and David returned to picking up the scattered papers, but it was not long before Abenray again spoke.

"You know, don't you, that I'm going blind? You've seen how I have difficulty finding my way around?"

"Yes, Maestro, I've seen your hardships."

Images flashed in David's mind of the times he witnessed him topple inkpots, knock over chairs, or grope in midair in search of a doorknob, or something else he needed.

"When I first understood I would in time lose my sight, I fell into deep anguish. I asked how am I to perform my duties as a scribe if I lose

69

the main instrument of my calling? I lost precious time wallowing in that despair."

David stopped what he was doing, approached, and sat silently at the old man's feet. "But you have other gifts, Maestro." He was thinking of his teacher's wisdom and deep faith in life.

"That's true, David, but a writer of letters, and a reader of manuscripts without sight is diminished in his calling. However, since such is my destiny, I've come to accept it."

"What can I do? Tell me, and I'll do it."

Abenray reclined into his chair, all the time combing his beard with his fingers, obviously in deep thought. With eyes dulled by cataracts, he gazed around, first at his worktable loaded with papers and documents, then over to shelves that housed even more of his work, and then finally out toward the flow of people crowding the street beyond his stall.

"What I want you to do is to pursue your destiny."

"What do you mean?"

"I mean that you and Zepyur must set out toward what awaits you. I cannot pretend to say I know what it is, but I do know you have a life in front of you, and that it is not here. So you ask me what you can do, and I respond that you must go out in search of that destiny."

"Maestro, I won't leave you. You need a helper, and as I said in the beginning, here am I."

Again, the old Jew fell silent, and David waited. In a while, Abenray sighed deeply and nodded.

"Yes, I need assistance, and you have been a good helper, and I know I cannot be alone. But, David, I have not always been alone. I once had a wife and two children, a daughter and a son. We lived in Baku where we had a good and prosperous life, but then, when the days of the oil richness came upon that town, men became mad with a greed and rage that incited them to evil. They often went on rampages, burning the homes and holdings of Jews like me. In the midst of that rage, my wife and daughter were murdered, but my son and I lived to escape, and we made our way out of Russia. We reached the village Yasamal where I left him with a family of the Ashkenazy tradition, where he has been living since then. We've remained in contact, and now he is a man on his way here to be my other self."

David was surprised to hear this part of his mentor's life, and he was happy to know he had someone to help carry on with his life. David had often wondered about his mentor's solitary life and how he coped with loneliness.

"Maestro, I'm glad to know of your son. Is this the reason you're not unhappy despite being alone?"

After a moment of thought, Abenray answered, "You're mistaken, young David. I have never been alone, neither have I been lonely." When Abenray sensed his assistant's dismay, he went on. "Being alone does not mean one is lonely." Then he became silent again.

Baffled, and not knowing what to say, David stammered, "Maestro, I'm trying to understand your words."

"One day you will understand."

For the time being, however, David did not understand, so he turned to what he thought more important; he was still unsure of what he should do.

"What would you have me do?"

"What I've just told you. I want you and Zepyur to continue on to Spain. However, I ask you to wait until my son arrives. I have money ready to give you so that you may travel safely."

"I've saved coin from what you have allotted me."

"All the better!"

Again, Abenray became silent, leaving David to ponder on what next should his and Zepyur's plan. At least one step was already decided, and that was to wait for the scribe's son to arrive, and then on to Córdoba. In the meantime, one thought flashed through David's mind.

I still have time to meet one of the forbidden women.

CHAPTER TWELVE

Another Secret

DOLORES NEVER saw her mother's smile again; not a real smile, one that came from her heart. During the last hour on the train, Dolores could hardly stop looking at Cele's face, wondering if that was how grown-ups acted when they were sad: very still on the outside, but maybe crying on the inside.

Esperanza's disappearance broke Cele's heart, but what could Dolores do? What could anyone do? In the beginning, she was angry with her sister for doing what she did. Dolores wanted Esperanza to come back so she could slap her, just one time, and it was years before this powerful feeling left her.

The train finally got to Nogales where the family gathered their things and left the train, moving as if sleepwalking; they couldn't believe what happened. They didn't talk or ask questions, but Dolores knew more than anything that they were afraid of what their father was going to do when he found out Esperanza was missing.

When they got off the train, they found a mass of people, shouting food peddlers and ruffians screaming out bad words just to make their way through the crowd. Cele was steady, though, she did not stop telling her children to hold on to one another, and she kept it up until they made their way to the edge of that stinking mob. Dolores was the first one to see her father and Sebastián, whose head stuck out above that blanket of sombreros. She was so happy she even forgot for a moment that they had lost Esperanza. In the excitement of hugging and kissing and crying, it was Sebastián who suddenly stopped to look around.

"Where's Esperanza?"

What followed became a blur in Dolores's memory, maybe because it was so sad, but mostly because her father, who at first could not grasp what Cele explained, wept bitterly until he finally understood that Esperanza was gone.

Once steady, he looked at the children and asked, "Did any of you see anything?"

"No, Papa!"

They answered with one voice, but when, for some reason, Ignacio turned to look closely at Dolores, she repeated, "No, Papa. I didn't see anything."

After that, Ignacio and Sebastián rushed the family to rooms they had rented at a boarding house, and from there, they returned to the train to go back in search of Esperanza. Although they didn't know where or when she got off the train, still, they hoped to find her or someone who had seen her. Dolores kept her mouth shut because even though she knew where her sister had gotten off the train, she decided to lie. She didn't know exactly why she lied, but once she had, she was afraid to tell the truth; it became another secret to keep buried alongside other bitter memories.

CHAPTER THIRTEEN

Los Cristeros in Mexico

DOLORES THOUGHT she knew all about her sister, but she didn't. On the day Esperanza first saw Regino Nájera, she fell in love, not with him, but with the Cristero cause. As it turned out, it happened when she first glanced at him just as he slipped onto the train alongside the Gómez family. In that instant, she felt she would love him for the rest of her life. Esperanza was that way; once she made up her mind about something, it would be forever—or almost forever.

When she gazed at Regino, she liked everything about him. She liked his face and his coffee-colored smooth skin with just the shadow of a beard. His nose was long and straight, like a prince, she thought, and his mouth matched his other features, broad and sensitive. When he took off his hat to wipe his brow, she caught sight of thick, brown hair combed back in a big wave, and she loved it right away. Her eyes drifted down to his hands, and she noticed they must have belonged to someone fine and thoughtful, a writer, or maybe an artist. Was Regino tall or short? Esperanza couldn't tell just then, but who cared?

As she stared at him, he suddenly looked at her, making Esperanza feel she had known him for years, not just moments. Their glances merged like two streams of water that come together naturally and quietly to become one warm cascade. He smiled at her, and she returned his smile, holding on to its warmth until she noticed Dolores staring at her.

Trying to hide her irritation, Esperanza's face snapped around to look out the window, thinking, *That nosey little sister sees everything. One day she's going to get into trouble.*

Afterward, as the train pulled away from Guaymas, time became boring. Days dragged by until one night, something took hold of Esperanza, a crazy impulse new to her—something she was powerless to resist. Without knowing why, she made her way to Regino's side.

It happened quietly and quickly. Without saying anything, they reached out to each other and held hands. She felt a surge of pleasure especially when her thigh touched his. Then the whispering began as if they had known each other since forever.

"I'm Regino Nájera."

"I'm Esperanza Gómez."

"I'm a Cristero, and you?"

After a few moments, she answered, "I don't know what that is, but if you tell me, maybe I'll become one."

"We believe the Church represents Jesus Christ on earth, and that no one, not even the government, has a right to take what belongs to it. We believe our priests and nuns represent Christ, and to attack them is to violate Him. In resistance to those attacks, we're ready to die, even though people say we're wrong."

Thinking he was talking crazy, she asked, "What people?"

"People like those on this train, especially the government. For that much, everyone calls us criminals and thugs."

"Have you killed anyone?"

"No." He answered in a disappointed tone, and then added, "But I know that soon, I'll prove myself. Viva Cristo Rey!"

She listened, still thinking that what Regino was saying was nonsense. She didn't admit it to herself, but as he went on and on, she began to change her mind; new ideas drifted into her thinking.

I wonder what it would be like to fight with a pistol in one hand, and a rosary in the other. It could be fun!

It took only a while before she impulsively murmured, "Yes. I'd like to become one of you! Viva Cristo Rey!"

Just like that! Esperanza was ready to put aside her doubts as well as her family, as long as it meant staying close to Regino and finding excitement. There was something in her nature that made it easy for her to convert. It didn't occur to her that she might, in time, regret what she was doing.

It was at the town of Santa Ana that the two beginners slipped off the train. It was easy. It was a quick stop, but it gave Esperanza and Regino just enough time to climb down and disappear into the night. She followed his lead, confident he knew where to find the Cristero safe house.

No one saw them get off the train, with the exception of a pair of glowing eyes in the dark. Little Dolores, who saw everything, was a witness to the time and place of her sister's defection. Apart from that, Esperanza and Regino went undetected as they made their way down the cobblestoned street toward the secret house until darkness swallowed them.

Perhaps what followed was to be expected. Esperanza embraced the Cristero mission with such fervor that she even put aside the thought of having left behind a heartbroken family. Once she followed Regino Nájera into that safe house, she wasn't assaulted by second thoughts. Instead, she plunged into the struggle to defend the Church, although she wasn't altogether sure what that meant exactly. Along with other girls, she listened to the instructions of *los jefes*, who taught them how to carry concealed side arms and ammunition, as well as the use of those weapons. She learned the importance of passwords, secret signals, and how to identify a fellow Cristero even when surrounded by a crowd, all of it under the noses of police and government soldiers. She soon took to that cat-and-mouse game, disregarding danger, always thinking the enemy was too stupid to be a threat.

Esperanza did it freely; she liked the adventure and risks, but there was something she didn't like about living among that ragtag pack. In the beginning, she was shocked by the intimacy, the constant sexual encounters that went on, not only in private, but in front of others, right there in the dormitories, where men sneaked in after dark to slip under the covers with a girl. It was something Esperanza had not expected of devout defenders of the Church. *What a pack of hypocrites!* She tried to ignore it in the beginning by looking away from the horseplay and touching, but she had eyes and ears; she saw and heard it when it happened.

Maybe it was because Esperanza was still too young and had been brought up too sheltered. Her mother never explained what men and women do when they sleep together, and the only incident that could have opened her eyes, more or less, was having witnessed the assault on her mother. But because it was so distressing and ugly, Esperanza had blocked out the memory of her mother sprawled out on the floor with her legs spread wide apart, struggling against those heaving male buttocks.

Besides, we killed him, didn't we?

But now there it was, in front of her, right under her nose. Those men and women around her were young, hungry, and driven by urges too powerful to overcome. Groping happened around dark corners, sounds escaped from stressed throats, secretive heaving and sighing. Esperanza was aware of it all, although she tried to look away, or even plug up her ears. Sex happened, and it happened mostly at night when she heard sneaky footsteps making their way into whatever rooms were used for sleeping.

And then her turn came. It happened not long after she joined the movement, one night when Regino Nájera crept into the dormitory where she slept. When she felt his hands moving under the coverlet, she reacted and pushed away his fumbling fingers, but he pushed back as he climbed on top of her.

"Keep quiet!" His voice, husky with lust, told her to shut up, but she didn't listen. Instead, she hissed, "We're going to hell! We're not married!" But it was too late. It was already happening. He was inside her, heaving, pushing, all along muttering, "The priest will forgive us!"

It happened almost every night afterward, although at first Esperanza hated the pain as well as Regino's insatiable craving. In time, however, she began to like the intimacy, until she grew to want it, and she hungered for the moments when they came together. Esperanza and Regino never married, but that didn't matter because she wasn't afraid of going to hell any more.

During the following decades, Esperanza threw herself into the cause even when the killing and suffering on both sides grew to be so grievous that after years, most followers, appalled by the horror, dropped out of the cause. When that happened, the Cristero movement lost its energy, leaving only a handful of followers clinging to its worn-out mission, with Esperanza still dedicated, impassioned, and undeterred.

However, her perseverance did not mean she had forgotten her family. As time passed, she began to miss them more and more, not so much in the beginning, but afterward, when years drifted by and regret took root, growing until it became the center of her thoughts. That's when her dedication to the Cristeros began to slip, and she tried to find a solution by turning to prayer.

I'll pray for them. I'll offer my loneliness to the Holy Souls just so my family will one day understand what I've done.

But those prayers weren't enough, and she had to admit that they were empty and hypocritical. That's when the longing to see her family, to hear them, to touch them, became overwhelming. Besides, Esperanza now had a son she wanted her family to meet and embrace. And so, just as easily as she had joined the movement, Esperanza left it. She packed a bag for her and her son and headed to Nogales where they boarded a northbound train. Regino, who had disappeared years before, wasn't there for them to say "Adios!"

CHAPTER FOURTEEN

Constantinople

DAVID WAS transformed the day he slipped into the tavern. When he walked into the gloomy place, cackling laughter, off-key guitar music, and rough, vulgar talk wrapped itself around him; and he wondered how people heard one another. Bearded, sweaty men with scarred faces, ragged clothes, and tattered hats crowded the place.

David did not like the smell of the tavern; it stank of rancid garlic, smoke, and sweat. He looked around, expecting someone to ask what his business was, but no one paid attention to him so he pushed his way through those lumpy, swaying bodies until he found an empty stool at a table already packed with men so drunk they could hardly keep steady on their seats. David noticed right away that some of them held onto women who sat on their lap; they, too, were drunk, or at least half-drunk.

David, nervous and not knowing what to do, sat openmouthed, looking around the room. The stink and grime of the place was disgusting him more each minute, making his stomach churn, and when he looked at the women closest to him, he felt even more disgusted; he saw that up close, they were not as beautiful as he had imagined. Their faces were painted grotesquely; their dresses were a ragbag of colors, worn-out ruffles and ribbons; and they showed off legs that were scrawny on this one, or fat like hams on the other one. But more than anything, it was those wobbly breasts hanging from faded bodices that revolted him the most.

What am I doing here?

David moved to run out of the place, but as he jumped to his feet, he felt a hand on his arm. "Where are you going? Aren't you going to invite me to a glass of our fine wine?"

David looked over his shoulder to see a black-skinned girl, a complexion that radiated the enticing aroma of chestnuts and chocolate. Speechless, he stared at her, wondering where she had come from, and as if guessing his thoughts, she murmured, "From Africa." His eyes dropped from her oval face to a slender neck, then down to the beginning of a deep cleavage, to covered breasts that promised to be firm and lifted. His gaze then slid down to a slim waistline; a simple gown covered her body from neckline to tiny, pointed boots.

"Yes, my lady. Let's drink wine, if you wish."

David's voice was thick with shyness and nervousness, afraid of not saying the right thing, all the time hating himself for taking so long to meet such a lovely creature. When she pressed against him to scoot over on the stool, he flinched, almost tipping it over, but he regained his balance. And then, when she sat so close to him that he felt the curve of her hip pressed against his thigh, he liked it very much. He smiled at her, and she responded with the most beautiful smile David had ever seen.

"Let's drink!" she murmured.

Then they drank and smiled and caressed. After that, he didn't know when, darkness closed in on him.

When David came out of the alcoholic stupor that had sucked him in, he realized he was sprawled flat on his back on sticky cobblestones. Despite the ache in his back reaching all the way up to his neck and head, he forced himself to sit up, rub his eyes to look around, but there was nothing to tell him where he was, or even how much time had passed. He looked for the tavern's sign, but it wasn't there, and then he strained to recognize anything that would point the way home, but again, there was nothing.

When he finally focused, he understood he had been dragged from the tavern and thrown into that gutter. His hand jerked up to grope his neck; he realized the purse he had tied there was gone. The beautiful girl was gone too. The ugly hags were gone. The vile, stinking men were gone. Everything was gone.

The narrow, winding streets of the Kasbah were dark and empty by the time David made his way back home. A few lights burned here and there, some at entranceways, others to mark a crossing, but except for him, the street was empty. He staggered and stumbled as he tried to hold his kaftan in place. His head ached, not only from the lingering vapors of the wine that escaped up his throat onto his tongue, but even more from knowing he had been swindled and robbed.

When he finally crept into the house, David went to the maestro's room, hoping to speak to him and spill out the evil he had done; when he entered the room, he discovered the scribe hunched over his desk. It took David time to understand something was wrong, but when he finally did, he felt blood rush to his head, making his temples hurt even more. He forced himself to move one step at a time, slowly, cautiously, toward his mentor; when he got near enough, he knew the scribe was dead.

Not knowing what else to do, David slipped his arms around the old man's shoulders and held him close to his chest. At first, he held him with eyes shut, praying he was wrong, that it was his imagination, but then sobs flooded his throat forcing him to cry out in grief, and tears rolled onto the lifeless head and beard.

David wept because he had come to love his mentor; he grieved because now the world no longer had such a man. Death had again come to torment him, just as it had with the death of his mother and the rest of his family, and so he cried. But most of all, David mourned out of guilt and remorse knowing that while he was locked in fornication with the mysterious beauty, his revered mentor might have called out for help, and he had not been there.

Hours later, as if in a confessional, David knelt on the floor facing Zepyur, but he confessed only those details of which he was least ashamed. He told of how he had become drunk, and of how he conversed with the young woman that had come to his side. He admitted there came on him a spell of darkness during which he remembered nothing except that when he awoke he discovered his purse was gone. He told how the thieves had torn his kaftan, leaving him even more ashamed and humiliated.

David, however, didn't reveal his intimacy with the woman, and he lied about not remembering. He kept to himself how that beautiful woman had enticed him to a secret corner and, there, opened his long robe while she inserted her soft hands into the most hidden recesses of his body. He didn't tell of the ecstasy caused by her caresses, neither did he confess of how she mounted him and then manipulated his private part into her own, converting them into one being. He didn't let on how she had incited him to plunge in and out of her until he felt the earth spinning around, then up and down, violently shaking him until he reached indescribable pleasure.

David lied to Zepyur when he said he didn't remember any of that, although he did remember, but his lie was so heartfelt that he wondered what was true and what was false. Now he was on the verge of doubting even the youth and beauty of the woman that had performed such a perfect act on him. Maybe she was an invention of his imagination? Maybe she was one of the other debauched women hanging onto pathetic drunks. These doubts sickened him because the more he thought about it, the more persuaded he became that the beautiful black woman was not real but made up by his imagination.

David's lies then became so entangled he couldn't tell where the truth ended and the lies began. He bent over, buried his face in his hands so ashamed he wished he could disappear.

CHAPTER FIFTEEN

Constantinople

THE LOSS of his mentor haunted David. It could be said that he mourned, and that at the heart of his misery was shame, an emptiness that hounded him, leaving him to wrestle with overwhelming loneliness.

How old am I?

Isolated, he struggled with the feeling that he was an old man. He sensed that his thoughts, his wishes, his waking hours were those of an old man.

I'm seventeen, but I know I'm much older.

It was under this cloud that, knapsack slung over one shoulder and Zepyur's hand grasping the other, David began the trek toward Córdoba. He knew what it meant; from the beginning, he understood that it was into the unknown that he and Zepyur were hurling, a journey riddled with dangers and risks of thievery, sickness, and even death.

On the other hand, David and Zepyur had prepared for this moment. Together they had stashed away a cache of money during their sojourn with Maestro Abenray while David gained the skills of an apprentice as well. *We won't flounder*, he told himself, and without looking back, the young man and old woman set out westward on an odyssey that would take more than three years.

From Constantinople, they made their way overland along the northern edge of Greece until they reached the coast of Albania. Once there, they rested for a time before securing a place on a fishing boat whose captain agreed to cross them over to the Italian coast. It cost them, but not as much as it did the other migrants and refugees taken on board, thanks to Zepyur who agreed to decipher the future of the crewmen as she read it on the palms of their hands. The boatmen, delighted with the prospect of discovering their futures, agreed to grant her and her companion a discount, along with much admiration and special care of the old woman. After that, the vessel made its way to Brindisi where David and Zepyur decided to stay.

"This city, David, is special. We cannot pass it as quickly as we have other places. You will see the reason, I promise you."

"You've been here?"

"Yes, I've been here before, although I cannot tell you my age at the time, nor what year it was, but it was with my father and mother that I first saw these walls and crumbling layers of what was once a glorious city. I remember also how moved I was to see how generations of people built new dwellings on top of ancient streets and walls, which, in turn, had been placed over even older ones. What I loved, and still love more than anything, were the most ancient ruins, and those people who have never abandoned what their hands crafted.

"What I mean, David, is that I felt the lingering spirits of ancient generations, and if I listened carefully, I heard their sighs and whispers. If you listen, David, you, too, will hear those voices calling out from the time when these streets were filled with Romans and then Crusaders and Muslims and Jews. Passing centuries have not silenced them. Do you hear what I hear even at this moment?"

David tilted his head to one side and then to the other listening for an unknown sound, but he heard nothing except the bustle of everyday living people scurrying from street to street, making a daily life for themselves. He heard only the present, along with a strong feeling of the soft breezes sweeping off the ancient Adriatic Sea.

"I don't hear what you do, Old One."

With a faint smile, Zepyur shook her head as she pointed toward the center of the city, deciding to keep her thoughts to herself, but as they headed toward the heart of the city, memories rooted deep in the cobblestones of those streets reached out to her and clung to her sandals. Zepyur understood. Transparent outlines of men and women from other times flashed before her eyes, skittering around corners, gazing down at her from rooftops, springing from narrow alleys, and even murmuring in now-extinct tongues. Ancient Brindisi came to life for Zepyur, a place where past and present joined, where the dead and the living inhabited the same space, swirling, moving, and interacting.

These are the spirits who century upon century, one after the other, were born, lived, grew old, and died here. They're still here, indestructible and eternal.

David tried but couldn't grasp Zepyur's understanding of the departed; for him, there was only the present and the living. What he did know, however, was that he would be her guide to wherever her path led.

CHAPTER SIXTEEN

Arizona

LIKE DAVID and Zepyur, the Gómez family roamed. Their travels took them through the Arizona desert, tormented by dust storms and heat, yet moving on from town to town in search of a livelihood. Sometimes the family lingered for months in this or that place; at other times, they stayed on for years. From Nogales, they moved on to Tucson, and then to Casa Grande, and from there to Gila Bend. Their last stop put them in Kingman where, in time, they finally saved enough money to cross over into Needles, California, but it took years for the family to get to this point.

It was hard for Dolores, Héctor, and Altagracia because they were yanked out of schools with all that moving, so they weren't able to learn much. The only good part of it was that they at least learned to speak and write English.

They usually settled on the fringes of those towns while Ignacio, Sebastián, and later on, Héctor, now old enough to work, found jobs harvesting lettuce, wheat, cotton; whatever crop was in season was the one they followed. During the off season, they worked digging trenches for the railroad, laying track, or whatever odd jobs came up. There were some seasons when they made their way to Colorado where the sugar beet harvests yielded bumper crops along with plenty of work.

Sebastián and Héctor grew stronger, more muscular with work, but Ignacio began to diminish, withdrawing and aging ahead of his time, but no one saw it; maybe it's because people don't notice what they look at every day. Nonetheless, he seemed to be shrinking, losing ground, just as Cele feared back at the beginning of their journey.

Pilar, and in time, Dolores, helped support the family by cleaning houses, but mostly by sewing for shops, or for ladies who noticed Pilar's talent for crafting fine looking dresses. For her part, Cele cared for wherever was home, while she did everything to keep a welcoming place for her family's return after a day's work. Most of all, it was Cele who held the family together, not only with the chores she tore into with energy, but by being Cele, angel and watchdog wrapped up into one woman.

But it was hard especially because the family roamed almost constantly during those bleak years when they hardly had a house; that is, a real house, much less a home. At best, they occupied rented rooms; once they lived in a garage for a long time, but they hung on, knowing their journey would end the day they reached Los Angeles, their final goal.

During that time, their dream to reach California came closer with each day, and they kept it alive by thinking and talking of California's golden sun, its ocean, and good work. "There, we'll make our real home." Cele made this promise almost every day during those last years in Kingman.

In the meantime, two of the family's members changed so much as to be nearly beyond recognition. Héctor was now about twenty, and Dolores was right behind him at eighteen; both had transformed not only physically, but they changed where it counted most—inside.

Héctor had developed muscles yet was on the short size, and he was cocky, always ready to fight. "Like a little rooster," people gossiped. He was contentious, resisting his father and mother at every turn, and he was lazy; he didn't like to work.

"I'm not a burro," he grumbled. Instead, he liked hanging around with the guys at the pool hall where they got hold of homemade beer whipped up in someone's backroom. Never mind it tasted like donkey piss; those loafers didn't care. They just gulped the stuff down while passing time checking out girls.

Héctor really liked doing this since he was now filled with curiosity about girls. "What's it like to touch those fine-looking tits?" He joked with his buddies, knowing that showing off always got him a big round of laughs from those loafers. It had to happen. The day came when Ignacio caught wind of what was going on with his son, and he tried to put his foot down as soon as he discovered that Héctor was slinking off to spend time with bums.

"That's it, Héctor! I forbid you to be with those good-for-nothings!"

But Ignacio had lost his place by that time, and the boy hardly paid any attention. How did it happen? No one knew, but as Cele feared, her husband had somehow lost his authority, and Héctor knew it. No one had to tell him; he just sniffed the air and knew it, so he didn't care what his father said. Instead, he went on hanging out with his amigos, getting drunk, and messing around with girls. Héctor was becoming a loser, and the slide became irreversible. His family seemed too wrapped up in the cloud of promise that waited in California to notice what Héctor was up to. They didn't see that he was moody and withdrawn whenever he was with them; something was eating away at him, but since he didn't speak up, his family saw the obvious but did nothing.

It came to an end late one night when everyone was asleep, and a banging on the front door scared them out of bed, all of them scrambling and pushing each other, trying to reach the front door. Dolores got to it first, but then Sebastián shoved her aside, opened it just a crack, and when he saw what was there, he threw it open.

The family crowded behind Sebastián, stiff like department store dummies, barely believing what they were looking at. Dolores, her face twisted with shock, stood next to Sebastián. Pilar scurried to a corner where Altagracia stood with her hands clamped on her mouth, her wide-open eyes filled with terror.

Two policemen held up a limp Héctor, barely conscious; his dangling head was wrapped in bloody bandages, as were his ribs. It took a few moments for Cele to come to her senses and reach out for her son, but one of the cops shoved her aside as they dragged Héctor to the couch where they threw him as if he'd been a sack of potatoes.

No one said anything; they couldn't. Instead, they stared, shocked by what was left of Héctor with his head wrapped in that bloody turban.

He'd been beaten senseless, and he was covered with gashes, cuts, and bruises all over his face, neck, and even on his arms and hands. One eye was swollen shut so badly that it looked like a rotten plum. His lips, too, were puffed, split, and still dripping blood. Although his ribs were wrapped, black and blue bruises already showed all over his chest where he had been kicked, and more than likely, bashed with clubs.

"Who did this to my brother?" Sebastián's voice was muffled, gagged.

"Hey, all we know is that it was two guys. We caught a glimpse of 'em before they ran off," one of the policemen spoke up. "We can't be sure, but it looks like it was the brothers of the girl your brother's been messing with."

"What?"

This time, it was Dolores who broke in.

"Yeah! She's one of those little Mexican chicks from across town. Your brother got her with a big belly." The second cop made a circular gesture with his hands. "You know. Nobody said she's pregnant, but we got eyes."

"Her brothers?"

More shaky words squeezed out of Sebastián's clenched jaw as Ignacio pushed against him.

"*¿Quién le hizo ésto a tu hermano?*"

Evidently, his Spanish jarred one of the cops.

"Hey, mister! Take it easy!" the cop yelled at Ignacio. "Your son is lucky. Those guys are nasty sons a' bitches, and nobody gets away with knocking up their sister. You might say he got off easy!"

"*¿Qué dijo?*"

Cele was finally able to speak up, although she was shaking all over.

"*Después, Mama, después.*"

Dolores tried to calm her down.

"Well, we did our part." The same cop, now calmed down, aimed his words at Cele. "We took him to the emergency. He's wrapped up, and he'll be okay, but it's going to take a long time. Christ! Just look at him! Well, good luck, and see ya' later. Tell the kid to keep his dick buttoned up behind his fly if he knows what's good for him."

Héctor was so beaten up it would be a long time before he could even begin to move; whatever California dreams he had crashed right there that night. On top of all that pain, he was now going to be a father, and even worse, he'd have to watch his back for as long as he stayed in Kingman; some families never forget whoever messes with a daughter or sister. But it was almost as bad for Héctor's family because now they faced having to put off their California plans.

No one thought of getting more sleep that night. Instead, they sat by Héctor, stretched out on the sofa looking like one of the departed, and they the mourners.

"Papa, what are we going to do?"

Sebastián broke the silence and glared at his father, expecting to get a resolution from him.

"What do you want us to do?" Ignacio was nearly in tears.

"Something! We can't just pretend Héctor wasn't almost killed. We have to show them we're not cowards."

"No! To do anything like what you're trying to say will only make things worse." Shocked by what Sebastián was implying, Cele broke in. "Remember, you have sisters! They will be the first to be hurt in revenge. No! Forget what you're thinking. Besides, we have to think of the girl. What about her? It was your brother who abused her. He's responsible."

Dolores interrupted Cele. "Why should we care about some girl? I say, let's leave Kingman right now! That's what we should do!" She was about to say more, but Sebastián cut her off.

"Shut up, Dolores! This isn't any of your business!"

"You shut up!" incensed, Dolores shouted back. "Who do you think you are talking to me that way? It's my life too! Why don't you ask me what I want to do? If you don't have the guts to leave this place, I do. I'm not going to give up going to Los Angeles just because of what Héctor's done."

Cele put a stop to the argument right away. Her voice was shrill and scared but filled with the authority that should have been her husband's, the man who now sat wringing his hands, jiggling his knees up and down, clearly overwhelmed.

"Keep quiet, the both of you! This isn't the time to fight! We have to think of what's right to do, not getting even, or leaving, or anything else foolish. We have to be calm and intelligent!"

Her words silenced her son and daughter; they sucked up the anger and alarm that had taken over when they saw Héctor's mutilated body.

"For now, everybody goes to bed! Tomorrow we'll talk and plan. We'll think of something."

The next day came, and Ignacio and Cele had to face it with bitterness in their mouth, as well as a heavy heart. Of all the heated words exchanged by the family the night before, it was what Dolores said that most alarmed Cele. She knew her daughter, and she also knew that what Dolores said was what she meant. Cele was not going to stand by and watch her daughter separate herself from the family because of Héctor's bad behavior.

Together they devised a plan to propose that Héctor marry the girl right away. It didn't matter that he wasn't asked what he thought; it was what had to be, and that was all there was to it. However, when the proposal was taken to the girl's family, it turned out to be a waste of time; they rejected the offer.

"Keep him! He's nothing but garbage. We don't want him to come near us, much less be part of our family."

"Fine!"

Humiliated and outraged, Cele, nonetheless, felt she and her family had done their part. "Now we can plan to make our way to California. We still need more money, but between all of us, it won't take long. That's our plan!"

Then, not too long afterward, someone plopped a basket at the Gómez front door; it was an infant girl with Héctor's features stamped all over her little face. She was wrapped in a tattered blanket with a wrinkled piece of paper pinned on it. Someone had scrawled in pencil, "*Mi nombre es Valeria.*"

It took time for the Gomez family to deal with the shock of Héctor's beating. On top of that, they had to get used to another child in the family, but in time, they accepted what they couldn't change; although the good feeling that had kept them going before was seriously damaged. Cele, however, tried to keep alive the goal that had energized her from the beginning, although doing this was especially hard because of the irreversible losses suffered by her family, now made worse by Héctor.

The loss of Esperanza as well as the hope of ever seeing her was a heavy burden for Cele, as was Dolores's growing detachment and her solitary ways. Above all, watching Ignacio descend into a pit of depression and isolation also broke her heart. And now Héctor! Still, she fought off sadness reminding herself that soon they'd be in California where every good thing was possible. She clung to that dream even now when she realized that Héctor wasn't the same; that maybe he would never be himself again.

She fought off that reality, she even tried denying its signs, but long after his wounds healed, Cele saw it every time he gazed at her with dim eyes and responded with imbecilic grins, showing that he was content to sit listless hour after hour. The signs were there for anyone to see that whenever he needed to go to the toilet or to bed, someone had to lead him by the hand. And the way he talked was mixed up, hard to understand.

Cele did everything to stay strong despite knowing that her son's brain had been damaged beyond repair, and that he was condemned to be an unthinking creature, never to treasure his daughter, never to recognize anything good anymore. She had to remain steady in spite of anguish for her son, or the recurring fear of homelessness, or the nightmare of a family left adrift and rootless. She had no choice but to be brave because she was now the head of the family, and they looked to her for the strength to reach the end of their journey.

CHAPTER SEVENTEEN

Reaching California

DURING THOSE years of wandering, Dolores Gómez developed into an eighteen-year-old beauty. On the outside, what people saw was a girl of stunning beauty, with a lean, tall, graceful body. Her skin was still olive-toned, and her hair was a mass of dark-brown curls. When Dolores walked down the street, people stopped what they were doing just to look at her; they couldn't help it.

The inner Dolores, however, was a mystery; no one knew what was going on in there. What those who knew her did see was that she was distant, quiet, and even melancholic. But that was okay, they said; maybe she just thought too much, or maybe she was just a deeper person than most others. One thing was certain: Dolores was complicated, whether driven by memories or pushed by hidden dreams; it was hard to tell what she was all about.

Had Cele been able to peer into her daughter's soul, she would have seen she was still tormented by the bitter memory of her mother's rape and the killing of the ugly rapist.

However, there was a deeper anxiety that persistently made its way into Dolores's thinking: Her father, his withdrawal from his surroundings, and sadness that never left him reminded Dolores that she was responsible. The rest of her family often wondered why he became more morose each day, but she alone knew that it was the loss of Esperanza that had broken his heart. And she, Dolores, could have prevented it. Couldn't she? Yet she hadn't, and knowing it pushed her in the same direction of her father's depression, when there were days she could hardly breathe because of the weight of dejection on her chest. So to save herself from these bitter feelings and thoughts, Dolores, in time, invented a dream that she was certain would come true.

I'll become a movie star! It's going to happen when I get to Los Angeles where I'll be next door to Hollywood. I'm going to be a star just like Mary Pickford or Joan Crawford. I'm in America now. I can do anything.

As the Gómez family migrated through the dust and hardships of Arizona toward California year after year, it wasn't work all of the time. Dolores and her sisters found time on Saturday or Sunday afternoons to go to the neighborhood movies where a nickel got them into two motion pictures. It was then that Dolores began to burn with the intense desire to be up there on that small screen, to look as beautiful as Gloria Swanson or even Greta Garbo. The feeling grew in her until it eventually took over; it was all she could think of, and she welcomed this fantasy, especially when the old pernicious sadness crept up on her.

Dolores adored the stars' glamour, their beauty, their sensual bodies, and the exquisite clothes they wore; and she wanted to be like them. She did everything to dress, walk and talk like those beautiful women up there on the screen. When her friends looked at her, they were quick to say she was just as beautiful as Lupe Vélez, and this made Dolores's dream seem more reachable.

When she first saw the movie *Ramona*, she sat in the dark theater transfixed. The lead actress, the beautiful Dolores del Río, moved in such a sultry way, spoke so intimately that she, Dolores Gómez knew this was what she would become; she knew what she was going to do with her life. After seeing the movie a third time, she made up her mind: *I'm going to be the next Dolores del Río! Why not? She's Mexican. I am too. She learned to speak English. I already have learned it. She's beautiful. So am I.*

While Dolores worked, or walked to the store to buy groceries, or cleared the table at home, her imagination conjured up different settings. One of her favorites was of being chauffeured to the premier of her latest movie at Hollywood's Grumman's Chinese Theater, right there where her foot and handprints were cast in concrete alongside those of Lillian Gish, Ramón Novarro, and other luminous stars. In her dream, she would get off the limousine, and wild cheering from adoring fans would greet her. And there she would stand: bright spotlights focused on her showing off in a slinky, sexy gown, with a fur coat hanging on her slender shoulders; her handsome co-star suited up in a tuxedo, holding her gloved hand. She would blow kisses in every direction as she walked the red carpet into the vast, stupendously beautiful theater.

On the other hand, daydreaming of herself as a movie star wasn't everything for Dolores. Much of the time, her thoughts focused on her surroundings, and that was when she looked carefully at the American girls that rode the bus, walked up and down the town's main street; white girls who went in and out of the ice cream parlor hanging on to a boyfriend's arm. Dolores observed those girls and tried to imitate the way they walked and talked.

If those American girls she admired and envied so much left home when they reached eighteen, if they got apartments and jobs, if they made friends and paid their own bills, why couldn't she do the same? She envied those blond girls who walked along the sidewalk holding hands with their boyfriends, laughing and smoking. She was especially crazy about how they sauntered around in short slinky dresses, shimmying their shoulders and swaying their hips, so sure of themselves. Dolores really liked that, but she especially envied their freedom.

I will be like them!

Thinking this way energized her and yanked her out of her depression whenever she drifted into it. Although she couldn't forget that becoming like those girls wouldn't be easy because there was her mother and Sebastián who stood ready to block even a hint of her behaving like a gringa.

Dolores never forgot this, and because, as she saw it, her time to break loose was getting close, she braced herself for the struggle.

I will be free! That's what living in America is all about. Everybody gets what they want.

Dolores repeated this over and over, but she did more than just coddle her dream; she planned and mapped out how she would reach what she wanted. First, she'd find a job to put her in touch with people who counted, maybe managing a smart dress shop in Beverly Hills, or even organizing the fashion section of an upscale department store where the stars shopped. Yes, that would work out just fine—no more cleaning houses or sewing dresses for her!

And if such a job didn't show up, maybe she would find something that would prepare her for her first role, something in dancing.

"Just look at Joan Crawford, how she dances like crazy!"

What about a job teaching dancing? Dolores loved dancing, and she was good at it too. Whatever it turned out to be, that first job would be the key to her future.

She was confident that once in Hollywood, things would fall into place for her. Oh, she understood she would have to work hard to reach her goal, but weren't those tools already there for those not afraid of hard work? How else had the stars she admired gotten to where they were?

She was a fan of magazines that told of how so-and-so came out of a small farm in Kansas, or Michigan, or maybe Texas. They were small-town girls, nobodies, weren't they? And what about the star that was discovered working the cash register in a restaurant in Hollywood? It wasn't a miracle, she told herself. It was the real thing. It was America.

These were the thoughts that buzzed in Dolores's mind when she finally planted her feet on the sidewalk in front of the house in Boyle Heights, a part of East Los Angeles on a hot windy day at the end of 1928.

CHAPTER EIGHTEEN

Nearing Córdoba

THE SOJOURNERS made their way across Italy toward its Mediterranean coast; once there, David scrambled to get work on a merchant ship, making its way to the coast of Spain. When he got put up as a cabin boy, he secured Zepyur's place by getting her to do what she did best. It wasn't long before they got off the craft on the shores of Alicante where they knew right away what direction to take to reach the final leg of their odyssey.

"It's that way, David." Zepyur pointed toward the west. "We will ask as we move along, and people will tell us where to find the city of the exquisite Mezquita. It rests by a river so powerful you will never forget it, and you will always remember its walls erected by the very Romans."

"Old One, how do you know so much about Córdoba?"

"I remember."

Without rest, Zepyur and David began their trek toward the setting sun; they made their way on foot most of the time except whenever a kind person came along to help them. One time, a farmer offered his cart as well as bread, wine, and sausage. Zepyur showed David's and her gratitude by foretelling the man's future as she read it on the lines of his palm. He wanted to hear more, he said, but he had to push on to his grove that was not in the direction they were following.

Zepyur and David's walking ended when a caravan of gypsies invited them to join them; they were on their way to their dwellings in the city, they said. This encounter became a blessing because those people soon to love Zepyur. Perhaps they recognized something familiar in the old woman's face, or perhaps it was the stories she told while they sat by the fire at the end of the first day. Whatever it was, it must also have been the way she spoke because her words resonated with certain notes of that gypsy clan's long-ago language. The way Zepyur spoke enchanted them, inspiring them to play their instruments and to sing and dance with more passion, just as their ancestors had done in the golden days of Spain.

The distance between Alicante and Córdoba is not great, but it took days for the caravan to make its way over rough roads and countless stops. Every day, however, was important for David because Zepyur took that time to give him step-by-step instructions as to what he was to do when they arrived.

"First, you will go to the river to pay tribute to its ancient memories of powerful kings, emperors, and caliphs that have come and gone throughout the ages. There you will sit by the riverbank to gaze upon the castle where the most Catholic Queen Isabel resided. Do you know who she was, David?"

"No, I'm ashamed to say I don't know who she was."

"The great Isabel was the most glorious queen of her world. It was she who brought wise men, captains, and explorers, and even discoverers to her court, making Spain the most splendid nation in the world. She was equal to Sheba, queen of Ethiopia and Assyria.

"Do you know who Sheba was?"

"Again, I'm ashamed to say that I don't know who she was."

"Well, I will tell a little about Sheba as well. It was she who crossed the vast Arabian desert to reach Jerusalem and meet her love, King Solomon. She did it at the head of a retinue of camels loaded with precious jewels, gold, spices, and frankincense."

David listened in awe of Zepyur's wisdom, but other thoughts troubled him. Although she had, from the beginning, foretold their journey to Córdoba and what awaited her in that city, he now struggled to understand how she could possibly have the power to foresee the future, and the more he thought of it, the more bewildered and troubled he became.

Why didn't I think of this before now? And why is she giving me information about Córdoba's past when we are there to meet something yet to happen?

Thinking of her death saddened David especially because she even told of where her end was to come.

"*Right there, on the altar in the heart of la Mezquita.*"

Why there, and nowhere else? David thought, and even more. *Isn't the place of our death a mystery to us all?* he wondered.

These unanswered questions tormented him, and so, although he felt held back by something he couldn't define, nonetheless, he decided to speak up.

"Old One, why are you so set on the place of your departure?"

Zepyur stopped walking to gaze at something beyond David's shoulder. She seemed to be hearing something, or maybe reading off a page in an invisible book.

"I've already told you. It's the place of my mother's own passing."

"Yes, but did she choose that place? Or was it because it was close to where she was attacked?"

"No, David! She departed at the foot of that altar because it was ordained from all eternity that it should be so. It was her destiny."

"Does that mean that it's your destiny also to die in the same place?"

"In my case, dear friend, it is my choice."

"But how can you be sure that you will die there?"

"I am sure."

"Will not your death be part of your destiny?"

"Perhaps. Now, enough chatter! Let us continue our journey."

Later on, Zepyur spoke more, and David listened intently to each word that passed her lips, hoping to decipher more sides of the mystery. He needed time to be ready and to understand; this made him glad they were taking so long to get to Córdoba.

"Once there, you will walk through the streets where the Jews lived, where they wrote books and made commerce." David was deep in thought when Zepyur's voice startled him out of his reflections. "There you will try to understand why such illustrious people perished. However, that part of the city is a labyrinth; its streets are narrow and difficult to pass."

"I'll lead you by the hand," David answered.

"Then you will walk through secluded jasmine gardens, as well as hidden orange groves planted by the wives of Caliphs. It will be at the edge of those walls and fountains that you will find yourself at the entrance of the Great Mezquita."

David's heart raced with each of Zepyur's words that foretold his every step through Córdoba's warren of narrow streets and secret gardens, and now he wished they would never arrive. He secretly admitted that he was afraid, but no matter how much he tried to rid himself of that feeling, it was useless; he couldn't overcome his fear. After a while, Zepyur left off, speaking for a few hours, giving David time to deal with the turmoil assaulting him. Suddenly, she picked up where she had left off.

"Once we reach la Mezquita, you will not waste a moment before you enter its forest of Islamic pillars and arches."

"I don't understand. What forest?"

"You will know of what I speak when you see it with your own eyes. Once there, you will search for a hiding place, somewhere in a dark corner, and there you will hide."

"Won't you be with me?"

"Yes!"

"What will we hide from?"

"Oh, there are custodians whose responsibility it is to assure the place is empty by the time its doors are shut for the night. However, it will be during the night hours that we will need to be close to the Christian chapel, and we can do that only by hiding. It will be you, David, who will guide me there to pass into the other world."

More talk of her death added to his sadness and confusion, and he felt his resolve melting away with each minute.

"I don't know if I'll be able to do such a thing."

"You will! From there, you will take my remains to a crest above the city, and there find dry wood to incinerate my body. You will then wait to gather the ashes and scatter them to the winds that blow from the great desert of Africa. After that, David, you will find the path that will lead you to your own end."

And as if discerning his growing alarm, she said, "You must not fear because I will be with you. You will never forget me."

Zepyur said nothing more that day until the caravan halted at the ridge of a low hill overlooking the city and the river. David's eyes followed its banks to several bridges, until his eyes paused on a castle. As if knowing what he was looking at, a voice sounded out, "There is el Alcazar, and the river is el Guadalquivir. Beyond that is la Mezquita!"

David's heart sank; he wished they were back in Constantinople, at the beginning of their journey, when he was still a boy and his innocence was a shield that kept away fear. But now he was a man face-to-face with his revered companion's death, and he had nothing to protect him against the terror overtaking him. He turned to Zepyur.

"I don't want us to go into the city."

"You must, David. It's your destiny."

There was that word again, but not knowing what Zepyur meant with it only confused him.

Does destiny mean I don't have a choice? Or does it mean that all that has happened, all that will happen in my life, were meant to happen at the moment of my birth?

David went on thinking, turning over questions and doubts in his mind while the caravan inched toward the city.

Why does she say "you" and not "we" when she speaks? Won't she be with me? How can she be sure of what I will do? Why is she instructing me, giving me directions, as if I were still a lost child?

David pondered and questioned, gradually understanding that perhaps her words were not instructions, but rather a prophecy. Could it be that this was the mystery that had bound him to Zepyur from the first moment he saw her sitting under the little tree outside the orphanage? Hadn't she even, at that moment, foretold their journey to Córdoba to meet her death?

"It's where I will die," she had said, *"where you will see that my remains are consumed by fire."*

Zepyur's words sprang back from where he had stored them in his memory, but he now realized that he had not understood the true meaning of her words because he was just a child at the time, one who saw things as a child, not as the man he had become. David, however, accepted that he must now fulfill the promise he made, that he now must rid himself of the fear that was grinding him down and be prepared to help Zepyur to her final resting place.

When Zepyur and David entered Córdoba to make their way through its labyrinthine passageways to la Mezquita, everything she had predicted came to pass. As she foretold, she expired at the foot of the altar, after which David put her remains to fire. When he completed the ritual, he scattered her ashes to the winds that sweep northward from Africa's great desert. He did this knowing in his heart that she now belonged to the mighty river and mystic spires of Córdoba.

With this last rite, Zepyur's prophecy was fulfilled.

CHAPTER NINETEEN

Ports Unknown

KNAPSACK SLUNG over his shoulder, David climbed down from that wind-swept hill to begin a trek south, and he did not change direction until he reached Cádiz. He stayed there a short time before he signed on with a merchant marine named *Enigma,* the ship that carried him to ports unknown. It was a long voyage, and in that time, he connected with peoples of different skin colors who spoke in strange tongues. During the vessel's many turns around the world, David discovered cities with ancient names, places filled with faded dwellings and crumbling castles, where he became drunk and brawled, played games of chance, won, and lost money. It was at those distant harbors where he made love to women in bordellos, in taverns, and in darkened alcoves, always remembering the black and youthful woman who taught him how to make love when he was still in the Kasbah of Constantinople.

Throughout his journey, David always carried the memory of Zepyur close; he often spoke to her, yearning to hear her gentle voice giving him advice. *"You will never forget me,"* she had predicted, and so it happened that he often spoke to her of his life and what its meaning could be. But when she responded, her voice was not always clear; at times, it blurred, and sometimes her words were spoken in an unknown language. So David wandered aimlessly without knowing the direction of his path, or where it would end.

By the time the *Enigma* reached its final destination at the port of Los Angeles in California, David Katagian was a twenty-three-year-old man whose soul was wise beyond his years. Now he knew he had finally arrived; this time, Zepyur's voice told him so. This was America, the golden land where all dreams were possible, where it didn't matter that he was Armenian, or that he had a long nose and bushy hair, or that he spoke funny English, or that he was born in this or that other village. The whole world knew this was the land where everyone had a chance to make good whatever he dreamed just as long as he worked hard.

It was 1928, and David had made it to Los Angeles with 150 dollars of back pay stuffed into his pocket, making him feel a rich man. He was ready! He knew that here he would find the right woman, and together they would create a family, and there was nothing to get in the way of his dream, of this he was certain.

It was America.

CHAPTER TWENTY

Dolores, Los Angeles, 1928

DOLORES AND her family piled off a dilapidated truck Sebastián had bought from a buddy in Kingman. The thing was a jalopy covered with chipped paint and a banged-up fender, but its paneled flatbed and engine were good. The best part was that it provided space for the family to travel together from Needles across California to Los Angeles.

Sebastián did the driving. Cele, with Valeria on her lap, sat between him and Ignacio up front in the cab; the rest crammed into the truck's rear flatbed, along with their things. They knew where they were going—Boyle Heights—Cele had an address, a house on South Boyle Street just where it crosses Sixth Street, close to the bridge.

Dolores, despite her fatigue, was smiling as she jumped off the truck and planted her feet on the curb thinking, *At last! So close to Hollywood!* Cele, too, was thinking but she kept her thoughts to herself as she shuffled off the truck's running board with the baby girl in her arms. Tired, dusty, hungry, but still together, the family stood in a row on the sidewalk, shoulder to shoulder, holding on to hats and jackets that flapped wildly in the gusting hot wind. Shielding their eyes against the setting sun, they gazed with curiosity, and with just a little bit of awe, at the place that was now their new home. They liked all of it. They even liked the patch of grass out front and the bushes lining the wide porch.

"A real house!" one of them blurted out in disbelief.

"Yes!" This time, it was Cele speaking. "Here's the letter saying our deposit is good, and that the house is ours for at least a month. Maybe more. Here's the key!"

More silence as heads turned to look up and down the block at the other houses and then down the palm-lined street toward Sixth Street.

"Look at the big building! It's a castle!" Altagracia wondered, "What is it?"

"We don't know, but I'll find out." Sebastián, fatigued by all the driving, was just as curious as the rest. "In the meantime, let's go in and take a look at the place."

The house faced west on South Boyle Street, an ordinary-framed house with three bedrooms, a nice front room and big kitchen, and it even had an indoor bathroom with a toilet in a big screened-in back porch. Cele got the good deal through her friend Inés; it even included a stove, icebox, and the house was furnished with a few other necessary pieces. Now as the family traipsed through the place, they liked it, not knowing it would be home for them and their descendants for many years to come.

"Let's get to work!" Wasting no time, Cele organized her family. "Héctor, sit here with Valeria. Don't let her walk away!" She steered her son and little girl onto a built-in ledge on the porch. "Everyone bring something in from the truck, put it where you think it should go."

"Mama, I'm hungry!"

"We'll eat when we finish. In the meantime, there's a bag of oranges somewhere on the truck. Find it, and eat one!"

Not long after the family settled into their new place, Sebastián got a job in construction, as did Pilar and Altagracia, who went to work in a dress and underwear factory. That left Dolores who, for some reason or another, refused to go back to making dresses.

"You can't stay at home while your brother and sisters are working," Cele urged Dolores. "You have to do your part."

"Yes, Mama. I know. Give me time to find the right kind of work. You see how I look in the newspaper every day to find the right job."

"The newspaper? What good is it compared to what your sisters can get you at the factory? Right now!"

It went that way for a long time until the day Dolores left the house early one day and didn't return until it was nearly dark; she was dressed up in a white uniform trimmed in blue. The family, already at table ready for dinner, stopped to stare at her, wondering what she was up to.

"She's finally gone crazy!"

That was Altagracia, two years younger than Dolores, the sister who didn't hold back what she was thinking.

"Shut up! I'm not crazy! Just smart! I got a job at a restaurant on Third and Hill. It's not much, but it's close to Bullock's, where movie stars shop and stay for afternoon tea. My next step is to get hired by that tearoom, and after that, who knows?"

Now they knew their sister had gone crazy, but no one said anything. They just stared at Dolores, all dressed up in that worn-out old uniform, but not ready just yet to let them know what had happened.

What happened was that she had seen an ad in the newspaper: "Waitress wanted. Good hours. Lunch free. Holidays off. Eddie's Diner at Third and Hill Street. Ask for Ronnie."

The place, Dolores discovered, was a long, narrow space, one side lined with tables for two, and a matching long bar with built-in stools on the other side. Overhead fans cooled it, and the floor was covered with sawdust. Because light came in only from one large front window, the diner was dim, moody, lit by overhead old-fashioned lamps. When her eyes adjusted, Dolores saw only a few of tables filled, and a girl about her age, with pale blond hair, serving them.

Dolores asked at the bar for Ronnie, who turned out to be a skinny guy with beady eyes that saw everything. He stared at her for a while until she spoke up.

"I saw in the paper that you're looking for a waitress. I want the job."

"Do you?"

The little eyes latched on to the unusually pretty girl standing in front of him. He took time to scan her up and down; he was looking for flaws, maybe an ugly mole on her neck, or a clubfoot she was trying to hide. He thought she was too beautiful for the job.

"What made you come here looking for a job?"

"I told you. I saw it in the paper."

"Right! You did say it. Well, let's see. Have you ever waited on tables before?"

"No, sir."

"Well, now, that might make a difference."

"The ad didn't say experience was necessary."

"Nope! It didn't." Spunky! He liked that. "Where're you from?"

"What difference does it make?"

"No difference! I just wanna know. So if you don't mind telling me, where're you from?"

"Mexico, originally. After that, I'm from all over the place."

"Aha! I knew right away you were different. I'll bet your name is Lupita or Lolita, or something cute like that."

"Close! My name is Dolores, and sometimes people call me Lola." Shoulders pushed back, she was beginning to show impatience. "So do I get the job or not?"

"Okay! Okay! It's eight dollars a week, and you keep the tips. You have Sundays and holidays off. You get your lunch here. So if you like it, we got a deal! Your job is to make sure these tables are cleaned off after every customer. It's up to you to take their orders, serve them their meals, and see that their coffee cup is always filled while they're still sitting. Another thing, you let them know we have beer. Five cents a glass."

When Dolores raised her eyebrows, Ronnie was quick to say, "I know! I know! Prohibition! Well, here's the deal. We bring it from out back. Our customers know what's going on, and they don't care. Is this a problem for you?"

"No! I don't care what people drink." More spunk! Now Ronnie really liked the girl. "If you like it, the job's yours, but you have to start right now."

"I'll take it."

"There's a rack out back with different-sized uniforms. Get one to fit you, and come out ready to work. That's Rosie over there. She can be a little grumpy, but she's okay. Make friends with her, and you're on your way." Ronnie smiled, making his face wrinkle up in a funny way. "Welcome to Eddie's Diner, Lola."

"Dolores!"

She muttered as she made her way through the swinging doors leading to the kitchen, toilet, cabinets, and the rack with four or five uniforms hanging on it. Ronnie followed, and behind him was the other waitress.

"Dolores, this here is Rosie. Rosie, meet Dolores. She's your new partner."

"Hello!"

The girls spoke, at the same time eyeing each other, checking out looks, age, and dress.

"Rosie, help Dolores with a uniform and then come up front so you can show her the ropes."

When Ronnie disappeared, Rosie took another look at Dolores and said, "I think this one will fit you just fine. There's the toilet. You can change there. I'll wait for you up front."

Dolores came out dressed in the uniform that was a good fit. Right away, Rosie took her around the place: "Here you get your glasses, over there are the pitchers and napkins and forks, and all the other shit you need."

Dolores giggled at the bad word but still kept track of all the tips the girl was giving her on how to take this plate to that customer, and on and on. Then the front double door swung open, and two men came in; both were wind-blown and hot.

"There're your first customers, kiddo. Relax, smile, and they'll love you."

And that's the way it went for the rest of the morning period until the lull between the lunch and dinner crowd came around. Rosie came to Dolores and took her by the wrist.

"C'mon, kiddo! You've done real good for a beginner. I bet you're pretty beat, right? I know. I've been there."

She led Dolores to a stool at the counter and asked Ronnie for a couple of Cokes. Without saying anything, he plopped down the small glasses with the *Coca-Cola* logo stretched across the top.

"Let's rest before the real chowhounds hit us." Rosie looked into Dolores's eyes as if she'd just seen her for the first time. "Where're you from, kiddo?

Dolores liked that Rosie called her "kiddo"; it had a friendly sound to it. At the same time, she, too, looked at Rosie's freckled face and figured that she was about her age. She saw that Rosie was taller by a couple of inches, her eyes were light blue, and her hair, worn in a wavy, short bob, was pale blond.

"I was born in Mexico, but I came with my family to the US. We've lived mostly in different towns in Arizona. Now we've come here to Los Angeles."

"Mexico! Wow! That's pretty far away. Me? My family is from Oklahoma. They came here a long time ago, so Los Angeles is really my city. I was born here. My real name is Rose-of-Sharon, but everybody calls me Rosie. Where do you live?"

"With my family across the bridge on South Boyle Street. How about you?"

"Oh, I have a room up on Bunker Hill off Sixth Street."

Dolores felt the old twinge of envy thinking of Rosie living on her own. Then the girls stopped talking and sipped their Cokes while they stored up energy for the next wave of customers. But then, out of the blue, Rosie spoke up. "Say, Dolores, do you like to dance?"

"Yes! A lot, why?"

"Well, maybe we can go dancing one of these Saturday nights out on the Santa Monica pier. The Avalon Ballroom is really keen. All the best bands play there. I bet you'd love it! Look!"

She suddenly stood up, patted the creases out of her uniform, and began to click her fingers in rhythm with her feet, along with humming and singing. "Hey, you! Yes, you!" Her outstretched arm pointed at Dolores. "C'mon! Let's do the Shimmy Sham Sham!" And then, with swaying hips, legs kicking, one foot pointing in one direction, and the other the opposite way, she flapped her arms wildly as she belted out, "Charleston! Charleston! Everybody's wild about the Charleston! C'mon, let do the beepi-di-doo!"

Rosie surprised Dolores so much she laughed out just looking at that blur of flapping arms and kicking legs. Dolores couldn't help herself, so she jumped off the stool and joined Rosie in the clickity-clacking of fingers, the kicking, shimmying, sashaying, and humming. Dolores forgot that she was tired; all she wanted was to dance more.

"Hey, you two! Back to work! Three customers just walked in."

Ronnie's voice broke the spell, but it was all right because Dolores was now reinvigorated and ready for the next wave of customers. She served her tables humming and smiling until her shift ended. When she got home that evening, feeling more tired than she ever felt in her life yet so happy, Dolores looked at the faces of her family as she walked in the door. But that was all right because she wasn't crazy; she was just on her way to becoming the movie star she knew life intended her to be.

"Where have you been, Dolores? I was worried."

"I found a job, Mama."

Before she turned to go to her room, Dolores dug into her uniform's side pocket and emptied a bunch of nickels and dimes onto the table. The tips for her first day at Eddie's Diner amounted to almost two dollars, and when Cele counted the money, coin by coin, everyone gasped. So much money! After that, there was no more talk of Dolores having gone crazy.

She fell asleep that night thinking of how much she wanted to go dancing with Rosie. The thought fascinated her. *But how can I? Alone? Without someone to make sure I behave?* Her mother or Sebastián wouldn't allow it, and she knew it. More than ever, Dolores felt held back by her family's old-fashioned ways. But if she lived with Rosie, she could do whatever she wanted, whenever she wanted, couldn't she?

CHAPTER TWENTY-ONE

David, Los Angeles, 1928

IN NOVEMBER, the Santa Ana winds, hot, dry, and gritty, blow hard in Los Angeles. They skim off the ancient floor of the Mojave Desert, snake over mountains and through gorges all the way down to the streets and alleyways of the city, drying up everything in their wake. Those satanic winds are unnerving yet marvelous to feel and see! The air over the city becomes transparent. To the north and east, nothing veils the mountains nor their giant crests; and to the west—if you stand on just the right spot—the vast Pacific ocean appears close enough to touch.

David Katagian, catching his breath, stood on the corner of Grand and Third Streets just where the heights of Bunker Hill begin. He turned in every direction thinking he was looking at a mirage: a shimmering city in motion; palm trees bending and swaying, fronds flapping; skittering paper bouncing on street pavement; flags beating against poles; dirt devils dancing from here to there; passersby, coats inflated by the gusting wind, walking as if floating, clinging to hats and purses. David squinted his eyes against the brilliant sun, thinking that down there, in the center of the city, even its buildings quivered in the wake of that transparent desert wind. Pitching and reeling in the wind, he loved Los Angeles from that first moment.

After making his way from the port to downtown Los Angeles, David walked up Third Street to this corner where his mate told of a rooming house. But David needed the address, so he dug through his knapsack, all the time struggling against the wind to get at the little book where he kept addresses, numbers, and names. When he found it, struggling to hold down the fluttering pages, he finally found what he was looking for: "*Cooper's Rooms for Rent, 210 Grand, Mrs. Cooper, Owner.*"

David looked around focusing on numbers, and after walking toward Fourth Street, he doubled back, crossed Third Street, and there on the corner, the highest point of the hill, was the address he was looking for. David gazed up at the house, taking in its ornate gingerbread woodwork, and the wide veranda that circled its front all the way around to its sides. Now faded and forlorn, the house had seen better days; its paint was peeling in places, and some of the woodwork was crumbling. The large house had three floors with turrets and dormer windows.

Feeling a little timid, David patted down his hair and walked up the stairs into a small reception parlor. The place was hot, Santa Ana wind hot, unexpectedly stuffy although the windows facing the street were open, and a floor fan buzzed in the corner. A couch and chairs faced a low table piled with scattered magazines and newspapers. Further back was a dark-wood counter in front of a wall holding up a pigeonhole rack. Between the counter and rack stood a woman, severe-looking, maybe even a little grumpy. She appeared to be more or less middle-aged, gray hair pulled back in a bun, and she was dressed in a cotton print housedress.

"Good afternoon, madam." David heard his voice, heavy with nerves and shyness. He remembered it had been some time since he spoke English, but he saw by the woman's expression that he had pronounced his words well, and that she understood. But he also noticed that her expression became sharp, beaky, her forehead wrinkled; and her eyes squinted as if she wasn't sure how to treat him.

"Where're you from, young feller?"

He listened to her voice and caught its unfriendly tone; this made David more uncomfortable. Maybe all Americans were like her.

"I'm from Armenia."

"Come again?"

"Armenia. I am Armenian."

"Armenian! Oh! Why didn't you say so to begin with? It's your people that collect garbage across the river in Boyle Heights, isn't that right?"

Because David didn't know what she was talking about, he didn't answer; he only raised his eyebrows.

"Oh yeah! I shoulda known. You have the nose and hair the rest of you have. Well, okay! I suppose that's where you'll be looking for work. You don't have a job, do you?"

"No, madam. But I can pay for a room."

She didn't respond, but for several moments, she glared at David while he shifted from one foot to the other. Although her pale blue eyes made him nervous, he could tell she was thinking, trying to decide. Again he smoothed down his hair and straightened his shirt, hoping to make a better impression.

"Okay!" She finally decided. "I have a room on the third floor, and here's the deal. You get a change of sheets and towels once a week, but you make your own bed and keep your room clean and floor swept. There's a broom closet on every floor, as well as a toilet and bathtub. It'll cost you two dollars a week, a month in advance for today, so that means eight dollars up front. It's expensive, I know, but I run a good decent house here. And by the way, no visitors allowed, and that means women especially. No shenanigans! If anyone breaks this rule, he's out on the street before he has time to pack his bag. And stop calling me ma'am! My name is Mrs. Cooper."

Mrs. Cooper spoke fast, forcing David to concentrate on her lips just to understand her. As he stared at her beaked face and listened to her brittle voice, he imagined a cackling chicken, but he politely nodded when she finished.

"By the way, what's your name?"

"David Katagian, mad—" He corrected himself. "Mrs. Cooper."

She handed him a latchkey. "Here's your key. If you lose it, you have to pay for a new one. You're in room 3A, up those stairs to your right. You're lucky. You have a good view of the city."

David took the key, put his money on the counter, and then bag in hand headed for the stairs.

"By the way, Mr. Katagian, there're good eateries down on Hill Street. It's not a long walk."

"Thank you."

As he climbed the stairs, David wondered what she had meant saying that his people collected garbage somewhere. Although distracted by his thoughts, he found the room; it wasn't hard since there were only three side-to-side rooms on the corridor. He went in, and right away, he liked the space with its single bed and nightstand; a pile of folded towels was placed on the pillow. There were just a few pieces of furniture, worn and scratched up, but in good shape. Nothing was broken, and although the room was stuffy, the air didn't smell bad.

David stood looking around, his bag still dangling from his shoulder. A hand basin with separate faucets for cold and hot water was built into the far corner; a small mirror with a drinking glass on a rack was attached to the wall just above the basin. Over there, under a large window facing east, was a desk with drawers; it wasn't a big desk but good enough for a person to sit, write, or look out at the city.

To the side, David had a wardrobe for his use. He opened it and found that it had a rod and hangers as well as drawers for his things. Right away, he unpacked his rolled-up clothes, sandals, two books, the cloak Zepyur had given him when he was still a boy, and then his most precious possession, a small pouch filled with her ashes. Then he went to the bed and sat. It was a good bed; already David felt better.

This place is good, he thought.

He pulled off his boots, got to his feet, and walked to the window and opened it. Hot air poured into the room, but it was clean; he sniffed it and picked up the scent of ocean. Maybe there was a little fog somewhere out there hanging over the Pacific. The wind was still blowing, not as intense as a while before, but it was still strong, still shaking the palms back and forth. David again felt that he liked where he was. He also liked that his window faced east toward the mountains.

He looked down Third Street flowing with early evening traffic going and coming. His eyes followed the long wide asphalt strip until it disappeared in the east, now shrouded in the growing evening darkness. David stretched his neck from right to left to get a wider view, and he saw the other streets parallel to Third, each one as broad and straight, all of them reaching the river that connected east with west. David was intrigued by the streets that were straight and laid in the direction of the four points of the earth. Then he thought of the curved, narrow passageways of Córdoba, Constantinople, and Brindisi, some of them leading nowhere.

November days in Los Angeles are short, and as David looked out the window, he saw the sky dimming, its blue was graying, and then becoming dark. Soon it would be night. Electric lights popped up first here and then over there. Car and bus lights combined with store and streetlights: blue, green, white, and red jumbled to finally create a multicolored carpet that stretched out in every direction.

From that window high on Bunker Hill, David looked out at the city; he was trying to find where it ended, where its final border happened, but he couldn't see its end. The city's lights went on and on until they disappeared in the darkness to the north, east, and south. Only the ocean, on the city's western fringe, halted the city's spread. In his travels, David had never seen such a boundless city, and at that moment, he was certain Los Angeles was spread out at his feet for a reason. He didn't doubt it was to assure him that this was the place allotted to him by destiny.

He remembered he was hungry and thirsty, but he was even more tired and yearning for sleep. He poured a glassful of water out of the tap, cautiously sipped it and swirled it on his tongue. He gulped the whole thing, went to the bed, stripped, and then stretched out on it. He fell into a dreamless sleep almost immediately.

He woke up next day feeling rested but famished. He left the bed, headed for the bathroom where he relieved himself, and bathed. He returned to his room, shaved, combed his bushy hair thinking he needed a cut, dressed, and left the house to make his way east on Third Street. As he walked, he calculated that he had enough money left even figuring in what he had used on streetcar fare and what Mrs. Cooper got. He needed clothes and shoes, but that could wait until he found work.

He pulled out the address where a mate had told him he would find work at a training gym next to the Olympic Auditorium. So headed in that direction, he crossed Hill Street and then Broadway, but it wasn't until Main Street that he walked into a small eatery where he ordered eggs, toast, and coffee.

As David paid the waitress, he concentrated just to pronounce his words well then asked, "Do you know how I can find the Olympic Auditorium?"

"Sure. Walk down this street to Alameda where there's bus stop on the corner. The driver of the bus can tell you where to get off."

As he waited for the bus, and even more while riding on it, his thoughts crisscrossed. He still missed Zepyur, even after so many years. Her absence had left a hole in his heart that not even all the friends he had made could fill that emptiness. But she had promised she would always be by his side, and he believed her. This thought gave him comfort.

Putting thoughts of Zepyur aside, he wondered what life had in store for him. Why had his footsteps led him to this country, to this city in particular, at this time? He wondered if he would find the good life people said was here to be found if only he worked hard. Los Angeles already had captivated him with its people from all sides of the world.

"Olympic Auditorium!"

The bus driver turned in his seat to signal David who then jumped off the bus onto the curb to feel the wind blowing again. He hunched his shoulders, pulled up his collar, and looked around at the long row of concrete buildings.

His pal had said, "Close to the auditorium you'll find the training center called Shorty's Gym. Go in and ask for Shorty! Tell him you're my friend."

Hesitating when he first walked into the place, David took a few seconds to get used to the sweat-soaked air. When his eyes adjusted, a vast room with a boxing ring in its center came into focus. Two boxers were sparring; he could hear the grunting and muffled thuds of landing blows. He looked beyond the ring where there was equipment for lifting, pulling, jumping, and punching, all of it used by mostly young men—some still boys. The place was filled with shouting, arguing, guffawing, along with clanking weights. Above the din, a radio blasted out Bessie Smith singing something about feeling blue.

"What's up?"

David was startled by a rough voice that came from behind him. He turned to find a man, dressed in gym clothes and tennis shoes, looking at him with suspicion. David figured the man was more or less his age and height; his skin was dark brown and his eyes were even darker.

"I want to speak to Shorty."

"Who are you?"

"My name is David Katagian."

"From Boyle Heights?"

"Coño!"

A curse word he learned from a Cuban mate years before slipped out.

"Don't tell me you're Cuban!"

"No! I'm from Armenia."

"Shit! Where the hell is that?"

"Near Syria."

"Christ! All right! Enough of this talk! I'll see if Shorty's around, but you have to tell me more. What do you want?"

"Work!"

The man took a couple of steps back to take a better look at David.

"Hmm! I'll tell him."

With that, the man turned to walk away, but David stopped him.

"Wait! What's your name? I told you mine, now you tell me yours."

"Ricky Maldonado."

"Are you from here?"

"Yeah! I was born across the river over in East LA. Wait here! I'll try to get Shorty."

David nodded and stood back waiting, his eyes again pasted on the sparring boxers. He was thinking that he could do it just like them. "Maybe even better."

"Hey, man! What's up?"

David spun around to look at a man twice his age. He had expected a man of shorter build, but instead the man was David's height. Like Ricky Maldonado, the man was very dark-complexioned, muscular, and spoke with a gruff voice, but unlike Maldonado, this man was dressed in a suit.

"I'm David…"

"Yeah, yeah, I know!" He didn't let David finish. "What kind of work can you do?"

David, not wasting words either, pointed at the boxers in the ring. "I can do that. I'm good with my fists."

"Is that so?"

The man took a long look at David, up and down, obviously taking a measure of him. Then he grabbed his hands by the wrists, stretched out his arms, pulled up his sleeves, and looked hard, all the while turning David's arms, pushing them up and down.

"Close your hands! Make a fist!"

David obeyed and saw the muscles on his forearms bulge up. The man loosened his grip, and David put his arms down, looking at the man's face, trying to guess what he was thinking.

"Will you do it right now? I gotta see what you're made of."

Although taken by surprise, David blurted out, "Okay!"

In minutes, he was standing in the middle of the ring, wearing boxer pants, shoes, and headgear. David's heart was racing, but he ignored it even when he saw that his opponent was taller, more muscular, and had long arms. Suddenly and without warning, the man rushed toward him. David braced and raised his arms in defense, but the hits came down fast on his head, face, shoulders, and belly with the speed of pistons; those arms were a back-and-forth blur.

David did his best to fight back. He ducked, swerved, lunged, danced around, and sometimes landed a lucky blow here and there, but his opponent was made of iron, or something like it. Far away, David heard muffled shouts: *Jab! Jab! Duck! Move in! Use your right! Punch the shit outta the guy!*

Who were they prodding? Him or his opponent? Who knew? It didn't matter because it was no good; it wasn't working for David. No matter how hard he hit back, nothing happened to the guy; his blows kept coming. Suddenly, a left-right uppercut struck. *Bam-bam!* And then everything went pure black.

When David woke up, he was in a small room; its walls were lined with lockers. He was lying flat on a cot, and someone had put a bag of ice on his forehead, but it took time for him to get his brain and mouth to work.

He thought, *Coño! My head hurts!* Then he got his mouth to move, "What happened?"

"The guy knocked you on your ass, that's what happened!" Shorty stood looking down at David, his hands stuffed into his pockets. "But the job's yours anyway."

"What?" David was sure his hearing was damaged. "What do you mean?"

"I mean you've got balls! That counts more than long arms any day for a sparring partner. The job's yours."

CHAPTER TWENTY-TWO

Intersecting Paths

WHEN SHE walked in from the gathering darkness, Dolores found her father sitting with his eyes closed.

"Hello, Papa."

Ignacio looked up and gave his daughter a limp smile. Dolores didn't pay much attention to her father's apathy; she was drained, not so much from work, but from the experience with the stranger. She walked into the kitchen where she found Cele.

"Hello, Mama. "

"Hello, Dolores You're here a little early. Good…"

Dolores wasn't in the mood to talk, or anything else, so she said, "Mama, I'm tired. I'm going to bed."

"Don't you want to eat with the rest of us? Your brother and sisters will be here soon."

"I'm not hungry."

Her mother looked at her. "Stay with me a while. Let's talk."

"Okay."

Dolores gazed at her mother while she worked at the sink. She knew right away that Cele had something on her mind.

"I'm worried."

"About what, Mama"

"About you."

Cele leaned against the counter, rubbing her hands on her apron as if she had washed them and they needed drying.

"You've become so different. Sometimes I feel you're somewhere else even though you're in the same room with me."

Dolores wrinkled her forehead as she listened, and at the time, she pulled a chair away from the table. "I don't know what you mean, Mama. Are you saying you don't think I'm a good daughter?" She sat down.

"Oh no! That's not what I mean. You *are* a good daughter. You help out with the money you get from work, and you're obedient."

"Then what is it, Mama?"

Cele shook her head. "It's something I feel. I can't tell what it is, but I feel it. You're so different from your sisters."

She wiped her now wet hands again on her apron. At the same time, she, too, pulled a chair near Dolores. She wanted to be close to her daughter so she reached out, cupped her hands under Dolores's chin, and looked into her eyes. Both women stayed quiet for a long time.

"Mama, you know I'm not like my sisters." Dolores finally spoke up. "You know I can't be like them."

"What do you mean?"

"I can't explain. I'm just different, that's all."

"They're good girls!"

"I don't mean to say they're not good. I'm only saying I'll never be satisfied with the kind of work they do. Never!"

Dolores didn't mean it, but her tone gave her mother a message she hadn't meant.

"Do you look down on them because they work in a factory?" Cele's hands dropped from her daughter's face, and her expression became hard. "Remember, Dolores, being a waitress is no better than a seamstress. You must not put on airs."

Dolores realized that their conversation was going in a way she didn't mean it to, so she tried to explain, hoping her mother would understand what she was trying to say.

"No, Mama! I don't mean that. What I'm saying is that I'm a waitress now, but that soon I hope to be something else. I want more!"

Cele, not understanding, shook her head as she looked away from Dolores. She, too, realized their conversation was falling to the side of what either one meant.

"All I want for my daughters is happiness, Dolores. I want their lives to be better off, less painful than mine, but not at the expense of forgetting who they are, nor their beginnings."

"How can we do that?"

"Oh, in this country, it's very easy to do. Dolores, you come from us, and you must not forget it."

Dolores was struggling to grasp what her mother's words meant. She understood each one, but she didn't get what was really behind them.

"Mama, I want to become something special and different. If it means I have to change, I will. I'm not going to stay like my sisters."

Cele understood Dolores, and she felt not only confounded but also apprehensive.

"When you marry and have children, you will understand."

"No, Mama, I don't want to get married or have children, not until I reach my dream."

"Your dream? What are you talking about? Life is real, not a dream!" Cele got to her feet, now truly disturbed by Dolores's words.

"Dolores, let's not talk anymore. I have to be ready for your brother and sisters. They should be coming soon."

Dolores went to the bedroom, hoping her sisters wouldn't come until she was asleep. She stripped off her uniform, kicked away her work shoes, put on a nightshirt, and then flopped onto her narrow bed. She didn't bother to brush her teeth, rinse off her face, or other things she routinely did; she needed to reach the bathroom for that much, and that meant facing everyone in the kitchen. Instead, she turned off the light and fell into a deep sleep.

Not far from where Dolores slept, David sat in his room. He was deep in thought. He liked his new life, although he was sometimes lonely. The hole left in his life by Zepyur's death lingered, but what was he to do? Whenever the old feeling cropped up, he put it aside to look at other parts of his new life. It was only a short time since he arrived, but David felt he was a part of Los Angeles already.

There was something that helped him blend in; change came to him with ease. It might have come from his days in the orphanage when he learned that to survive he had to become like the others. Or perhaps it came from his travels with Zepyur when, for the sake of safety, he was forced to blend in with the hordes of ragtag travelers surrounding him. Or it might have been his peculiar ear that picked up different languages, letting him sound like everyone else right away. Whatever it was, David was now indistinguishable from the throngs that flocked to Los Angeles from all parts of the world. He became a native, and it came around fast.

One of the first things that happened to him as a result of that ability was that his job at the gym expanded from sparring mate to training program supervisor. It was a quick promotion, and he took it graciously, without questioning, mostly because the new job paid well, enough for him to save every week.

Next came staying on in Mrs. Cooper's rooming house where he made friends and got to know the neighborhood. The same was true at the gym where Ricky Maldonado, especially, became a buddy who showed him around. On Friday nights, they headed out to one of the speakeasies on Main Street, the ones that asked for a password. The two men usually had a good time drinking beer or whiskey or both, chatting and listening to jazz while getting tipsy. On Saturday nights, they headed to either Venice or Santa Monica to dance and make friends with girls. As it turned out, David was a pretty good dancer, and girls didn't give him the brush off, although he was a little on the short side.

He was quick to catch on that to be like everyone else he needed to look the same. So he put thirty dollars aside and found a little shop on Spring Street where he bought a suit along with extra slacks, dress shoes, shirts and ties, a striped blazer, and one of those popular straw hats. All dressed up, David looked in the mirror, and he liked what he saw, maybe not tall enough, but not bad-looking, and for sure not different from others who strolled up and down Third Street.

So when the old feeling of loneliness crept up on him, David looked around and reminded himself that life was good, not only for him but for most everybody. On top of that, times were good during that last part of that year. There were plenty of jobs to pick from and decent places to live in, so he felt good.

The year was ending. Every time David stepped out, he was amazed to see how people in this part of the world celebrated December with little trees covered in lights set up in windows. The season's joyful spirit also moved him; people planned parties and get-togethers for any reason, especially for the big party to end the year. Soon it would be 1929, and because it was to be the last year of the decade, everyone said it was special. The years to follow would surely be even better; at least, it's what everyone expected.

But something else had slipped into David's new life, something that made his spirit soar even more than dancing or drinking or making friends. He had seen a girl, a waitress, someone he couldn't get out of his mind since the first moment he saw her. *She's the most beautiful woman I've ever seen*, he murmured. Not even his Constantinople lover compared with this olive-complexioned beauty.

David had not spoken to her; he didn't even know her name—not yet—but he knew she would be the love of his life. He felt this the first time he saw her. For the time being, however, he was content to just gaze at her from a corner of the diner where he took his meals.

It was because of her that David became a regular customer at Eddie's Diner for breakfast and dinner. Every day, when he left the place, he found his thoughts filled with her slender body, her beautiful face, the mass of dark brown curled hair that crowned her head and her glorious eyes. She was the last thing he thought of before falling asleep, and the first when he awoke. In between every thought, what he really wanted with all his heart was to get to know her and make love to her.

But there was a problem. It turned out that no matter how intensely David gazed at the girl's face whenever she came to his table, not once did she return his look. It discouraged him, but he decided to wait, content for the time being to just look at her when she came to take his order and fill his coffee cup. *When she looks into my eyes, she will see my love*, He said this to himself all day long, convinced the girl would love him in return, although it hurt him to see how standoffish she was.

David's turmoil went on until one evening when he stepped into the diner and headed for his table. When his eyes adjusted to the dim light, he saw the girl standing at the counter alongside the other waitress; they were chatting. As soon as he sat down, the blond one turned in his direction; gave him a long, cocky look; and then turned to say something to his beloved. He couldn't hear, but he sensed she was saying something about him. And he was right.

"Kiddo, the guy's back, and there he goes all over again, just staring at you. One of these days, he's gonna go cross-eyed."

Rosie, seeing Dolores's unease, rubbed it in by crossing her eyes, and flashing a huge grin. Still, Dolores refused to look in David's direction, pretending to fuss with napkins and forks.

"C'mon! At least give him the glad eye! You know, the old wink-wink! It works like a charm."

"I don't like him!"

"Why? I think he's kinda cute. A little on the short side, but okay."

"His nose is too long."

Dolores kept on folding napkins, trying to look composed, and much too sophisticated to even notice someone like David.

"Shit! Who do you expect to walk into this dump, Rudolf Valentino? You're not gonna get a movie star in this place! No, sir! Not in a million years!"

Mention of the famous movie star jarred Dolores, and only then did she turn to look at David, who caught her look, and it made his hand jerk so badly he pushed a knife and fork off the table. The loud clanking made close-by customers turn and stare at him. Embarrassed, David ducked under the table as if to pick up the stuff, but he was really trying to hide.

"Kiddo, that's it! Go help him, and be nice. Who knows, maybe he's a good dancer. I've already met his pal, a Ricky something-or-another, and we liked each other right away. Try it! It might work out for you too."

That did it! Dolores dropped what she was doing, reached for her pad with one hand, and a coffee thermos with the other. She made her way to David who sat looking sheepish and squirming in his chair.

"Hello."

"He-hello," David stammered, but soon recuperated. "I'm sorry. I didn't watch what I was going."

"It's all right. Do you want some coffee?"

"Yes, thanks!"

"Milk? Sugar?"

"Yes, please!"

"What's your order?"

"Lamb chops, mashed potatoes, and gravy."

"I'll be back."

"Thanks!"

David couldn't believe what was happening. Was he dreaming? She spoke to him and even looked into his eyes. *Did she see what's in my heart?*

Dolores did see the fire in his eyes, and although she didn't understand what she saw, she sensed that it was something powerful. Confused, and at the same time beguiled, she returned to the counter to fold more napkins, and because Rosie had gone to serve customers, she was left to her thoughts.

"Order for table no. 3 is ready!"

Jarred out of her musings by the cook's loud voice, Dolores got the plate along with a side of sliced bread and took it to David's table. He looked up at her, smiled, but didn't say anything; neither did Dolores, who went on to wait on other tables. She lost track of time, but when she looked over at David's table, he was gone.

On the bus that evening, Dolores swayed along with the bus's side-to-side motion, thinking of the young man who looked at her as no one had ever done. *He didn't even give me his name.* She crinkled her brow. *But I didn't give him my name either.* Yet she couldn't stop thinking of him, especially his eyes.

By now, Dolores was used to men staring at her; she was familiar with what was buried in those eyes, the ones that slid up and down her body, even the looks that undressed her, but she had learned to disregard those glances along with the uncomfortable sensation they gave her. Today, however, was different. The stranger's eyes were filled with light, nothing else; they gave her a feeling unlike anything she had felt before.

Funny, she thought, *I've seen him so many times there at the diner, but I've haven't paid him attention. Today was different. God! Why didn't I ask him his name?*

Dolores relaxed even more with the stop-and-go of the bus. She gazed out the window at people skittering along the sidewalk, holding packages and children, and she was aware of cars moving along with traffic. She was at the same time thinking of the effect the stranger's eyes had had on her, although she couldn't explain it. She felt different. *Thinking of him is making me think in a different way.*

The bus stopped and opened its doors; a woman came aboard, a man jumped out, and Dolores fell deeper into her thoughts. The stranger's eyes got her thinking of how she used her eyes. She remembered how she had used her eyes to spy on her sister Esperanza when they were on the train. Dolores watched as her sister got off the train with the stranger that night and did nothing. Would her father's life be more tolerable if she had told him where to look?

"Miss? Isn't this your stop?"

Startled out of her musing by the driver's loud voice, Dolores glanced out the window to make sure it was her stop. "Yes, thanks!" She got to her feet, skipped down the shallow steps, and out the bus's opened doors. When it lurched away from the curb, Dolores felt a little dizzy, so she sat on the bench while she got back her balance. It was growing dark; streetlights were popping on, and cars had turned on their headlights.

Her thoughts turned to her childhood years when she wandered through Arizona's towns and deserts with her family, and although she couldn't remember if she liked or disliked those times, she did remember so much of what she saw. She remembered, too, how she envied the white girls in those places because they were glamorous and free. And how did that jealousy creep into her? *It got in through my eyes, and it cut deep into me.*

Dolores sighed, got to her feet, went to the light signal and waited to cross Sixth Street. Traffic was heavy, but she didn't pay attention to it or anything else; she was thinking of the stranger's eyes again and what they made her feel.

CHAPTER TWENTY-THREE

"*WILL YOU* walk with me when you're finished?" David asked as she brought his order.

"Yes."

Cup after cup of coffee, David waited until Dolores's shift ended, and he watched her take off her apron and grab her jacket and purse to finally meet him at the door. It was their first time so when they looked at each other, it was with a shy smile; neither could think of what to say. They were quiet as they walked down Third Street toward Broadway until they reached a bus stop bench where they decided to sit and tell not only their names, but also more, just as if they had known each other for a long time.

David told Dolores about his family life in Armenia, how the family perished, of the years he spent in the orphanage, and of his travels with a wise old woman named Zepyur. However, he held back the most important part of his past life. He didn't say that in his travels, he had gambled, got drunk, indulged in hashish, and whored with unknown women. And most grievous, he kept his most shameful secret: that when he was still a boy, a grown man had sexually touched him and taken his pleasure from him, not once but many times, and that he, David, had murdered him.

Dolores opened up to David as well, telling about the small town in Mexico where she was born, about the revolution that swept over it, and how that war forced her family to abandon their home. She quietly told him about how she and her family wandered the Arizona desert for years, and she spoke even about the disappearance of her sister; but like David she, too, kept her secret. She held close her mother's shameful rape, and how she and her sisters had murdered of the attacker.

Then slowly, cautiously, she plucked up the nerve to tell David of her dream of getting to be a movie star. When she told this part, she waited, expecting him to laugh at her. Instead, he said, "Why not?" and then, as if sensing her thoughts, he added, "You're beautiful, more than any movie star I've ever seen! More beautiful than Norma Shearer or Tallulah Bankhead."

Thrilled, Dolores looked into those eyes that, by now, held a grip on her. She saw the same light that had first captivated her, and she really believed he didn't doubt she could make it to Hollywood.

"I'm trying hard to find a way. I applied for a job at Bullock's, but I haven't heard from them yet."

"Why Bullock's?"

"That's where movie stars and directors shop. Maybe I'll be noticed if I work there."

"Ah! Well, be patient, Dolores. I know you'll make it. But what about me?"

"What do you mean?"

"Will you still like me? Will you still sit and talk with me when you're famous?"

"I'll always be like I am now."

He became quiet, imagining Dolores as a celebrated actress. She would be beautiful, of course, but would she be happy? Would she still be herself? He admitted he did feel a little bit afraid that she would be hurt somewhere along the way.

"David, tell me about yourself."

"I have my own dream too. It's to live in a little house with you forever." David flashed a huge smile and then added, "I think a car will be part of it."

"Is that all, David?"

"What do you mean *all?* If my mother and father, any one of my family, came back to this world to find me the owner of a house, even a little one, and a car, and a job, you, me, and our children, they would find it hard to believe. I tell you, Dolores, they would dance and sing with joy! That would tell the whole world that David Katagian was really an American!"

When he noticed her dismayed expression, he went on, "We can do it, Dolores. I promise you! In this country, it's possible. Why not? Look around, and you'll see that everyone has what he or she wants. Why not you and me? Together we can do it!"

David spoke on without paying attention to the look on her face, and he talked without guessing that Dolores was reacting to the smallness of his dream. He didn't realize that she found it impossible to picture herself living in another little house, like the many she had lived in as she and her family wandered the emptiness and children? But Dolores was able to erase the distressed look off her face and said nothing; she kept her disappointment to herself.

And so Dolores and David talked to each other, sharing only part of what they had already lived but holding on to their secrets, perhaps because it was too shameful, or maybe they thought the day had yet to come when they would reveal that part of their lives. For now, however, they sat on that bench on a busy Los Angeles street, surrounded by a milling holiday crowd, telling each other what they had never before revealed to anyone.

They spoke for hours without noticing buses coming and going, or that the sun had declined, turning the afternoon into early evening. Neither did they notice that they had fallen deeply in love.

After their first encounter, David became a daily customer at the diner where he waited impatiently for the hour when Dolores took off her apron, threw on her jacket, grabbed her purse, and headed for the door. From then onward, they became a couple as they strolled down Third Street to Broadway, gazing at Christmas window displays along the way.

They held hands or linked arms; that was all they did, although they felt the growing heat of unfulfilled intimacy, a feeling that got more intense each time they came near one another. Sometimes that feeling hit unexpectedly after a quick brush of fingertips, or when they were pushed against one another on the crowded sidewalk. Dolores felt that deep impulse, as did David, but neither spoke of it because neither knew how to describe the rush each felt, what it meant; or maybe because it was just too soon. Instead, they responded to that powerful urge by nervously prattling on about nothing until their jabbering got so meaningless that they abruptly stopped talking, and walked in silence.

Neither one could explain how their relationship had grown so much in so few days, but it had. It was as if they had been together from a time unknown; they sensed that life had somehow meant for them to come together here in this city, at this time.

Each evening their magical walk ended with Dolores saying something like, "I have to go home. They're waiting for me."

"I want to meet your family," he would reply each time.

"No, not yet."

"When?"

"Soon."

"Why not now?"

"I can't explain. We have to wait a little longer."

That's when they parted ways, she to hop on the bus, and he to make his way to his room at Mrs. Cooper's, all the while wondering why Dolores didn't want him to meet her family. David didn't like the thoughts that crept into his head when she repeated, "Later! Later!" They were ideas that made him think her family wouldn't like him, and it drove him crazy.

CHAPTER TWENTY-FOUR

EVERYONE TALKED about 1929 as the last year of a great, wild, boozy, jazzy decade—the end of ten years of big-time spending, flappers, gangsters, bootleggers, and bathtub gin. And the idea to welcome in that fabulous last year in a special way started with Rosie; she wanted the two couples to spend New Year's Eve dancing the night away.

"Look, kiddo," she said during a lull at the diner two days before the celebration. "These flyers are all over the place. Read it! It has you in mind." Rosie handed Dolores a folded, wrinkled-up paper. "Go ahead! Read it out loud!"

Dolores was curious, but remembering Rosie was sometimes reckless, even a little crazy, she hesitated. Nonetheless, she took the flyer and smoothed it out.

"A Night To Find Fame, Fortune and the Key To Celebrity!"

Wrinkling her brow, Dolores looked up. "What's this about, Rosie?"

"Go on! Read the rest."

She went on reading out loud: "A night of dancing at the Santa Monica Pier Ballroom New Year's Eve, Louis Armstrong and His Hot Five featured. One night only! Dance away the old year!"

Dolores stopped reading, but Rosie urged her.

"Go on!"

"A dance contest will highlight your good times. The prize for the first place winner will be a contract with MGM Studios, and none other than the Boy-Wonder producer, Irving Thalberg, will present the award in person. Sign-ups taken at the entrance."

"How do you like them apples, kiddo?" Rosie's excited voice broke in. "This is meant for you! I've seen you hoofing up the dust back in the kitchen when you think no one is looking. Kiddo, I'll bet anything you can win first place, and with your looks, the sky's the limit!"

Dolores's heart was racing! She saw right away that maybe this was the break she was hoping for, the way to reach the stars.

"But..."

"What do you mean, *but*? There's nothing to keep you from going up there to show all those dummies how a real star does the Charleston! Haven't you ever seen Joan Crawford doing it? Jesus, can she cut a rug!"

Rosie had misunderstood Dolores's hesitation. She didn't know her friend had mountains to conquer just to spend a night away from home, nor did she know the only way for Dolores to do such a thing would be to lie. And what lie could she invent good enough to be believed by her mother and Sebastián?

"How could I do it? It would be really late when I got back home, and everybody would be mad at me."

"Oh, I already thought of that much! You can spend the night at my place. I have a nice little sofa that's pretty comfortable."

"You don't understand, Rosie. My family doesn't do things like that."

"What do you mean? What's wrong with spending a night with a girlfriend?"

"No! It's not done."

"You're right, kiddo!" Rosie put on a sour face. "I don't understand."

Still holding the flyer, Dolores kept quiet; she was thinking. Now that she knew of this once-in-a-lifetime break there was hardly a chance she was going to let it pass. But how could she convince her mother and Sebastián that being away from them for a night didn't mean she was going to do something indecent? *"No! I have to lie, but it better be a real good lie. Something they will believe."*

"What're you thinking, kiddo?"

"I'm thinking you have to help me think, Rosie. What could I say to my mother and brother to get permission?"

"Brother? What the hell does your brother have to do with it?"

"That's another thing you don't understand"—Dolores made a face—"so just help me think, won't you?"

"Of all the screwy things! Anyone would think you're going to rob a bank." Rosie mumbled, yet her faced pinched up, trying to hatch a good lie. She was thinking hard. "Yeah! I know what you can say!" She spoke up so loud it made Dolores flinch.

"Why don't you tell 'em your friend, the girl that works with you, is really sick with the flu. Tell 'em that she's alone with no one to help her, and she's lonely. Say you're the only one to keep her company, help her to the toilet and fix her a bowl of chicken soup. You'll think of something else, I know. The point is, you need to spend the night with her, especially New Year's Eve, when she'll be lonelier than ever, what with everyone out there having a ball, and she all by herself. Isn't that the nicest thing anyone can do?"

"I don't know, Rosie. Do you think it'll work?"

"Sure, kiddo! I'll bet your folks are Catholics, just like mine, and they fall for that kind of shit every time. What do you think?"

"Maybe." Dolores wasn't sure, but then, after some thought, she felt it might work. "Yes! And even if it doesn't work, I'm not missing this chance."

"What will you do if they don't let you come?"

"Never mind! I'm coming no matter what they say. Nothing can stop me. It's the break I've been waiting for."

"Okay! Count on sleeping on my sofa! We're in business! The thing is, we've got a lot to do between now and then. First, we'll go to Lerner's on Fifth to get us a couple of cute dresses. They don't charge a leg and an arm there, so don't give me your old Bullock's crap! Today's payday so we can go shopping during our lunch break. Then we'll get us new shoes and stockings at the shoe store next door to Lerner's. After that, we'll be set to cut a rug."

Rosie, nearly out of breath after talking so fast, stopped for a moment and took Dolores by her shoulders to study her hair. She turned her around, took handfuls of hair, inspecting it until Dolores pulled away.

"What're you doing, Rosie?'

"I'm checking out your hair. Don't get me wrong, kiddo. You have beautiful curly hair, but you wear it in a real old-fashioned way. You need to cut it! You know, be in style just like in Hollywood. After all, you'll soon be a star, won't you?"

Dolores reached up to touch her shoulder-length hair knowing Rosie was right. It was old-fashioned; she had thought of it before.

"I don't know anyone that cuts hair."

"Well, kiddo, you're in luck, because old Rosie has the answer. My friend Gloria has a little hair shop close to where I live. She'll cut your hair tomorrow just on time to get you spruced up for our big ballroom blast."

Rosie stepped back to get a better look at Dolores. "Come to think of it, I just saw a picture of Clara Bow in a magazine, and you'll look just like her with your new hairdo."

She was so excited she was ready to start dancing right there and then, but instead, she mumbled, "Goddamn! Will we be knockouts, or what?" Then she went on, "You and your guy, me and Ricky, we'll make two great couples, don't you think, kiddo?"

That night, Dolores faced her mother and Sebastián with the lie made up by Rosie, and they, reluctant at first, believed it. Next morning, Dolores, with a bag filled with overnight things, told her mother not to worry because she would return as soon as her friend got better. With a quick kiss, she rushed out of the house toward the night that would change her life. Dolores was sure of it.

That night, the ballroom was decorated with confetti and streamers and packed with dressed-up couples. Girls were stunning in bobbed hair, exotic hairbands, and slinky low-cut flapper dresses; guys were dapper in bow ties and form-fitting three-piece suits. They danced slow and sensuous to Louie Armstrong's *Stardust*, skipped into "After You've Gone," but then went wild with his "Struttin' with some Barbecue," and his "Sunset Café Stomp," all the time following the beat of Louie's throaty voice and rhythmic trumpet.

Dolores and David danced through the night without restraint, feet stomping and kicking, hips swaying and grinding, shoulders shimmying and gyrating. The hall jumped with couples doing the Lindy Hop and the Shimmy Sham Sham, wagging fingers in the air as they bopped up and down to Armstrong's hot jazz.

These were the last few hours of 1928. Now was the time to welcome 1929, the last year of a wild prosperous decade, so why shouldn't they celebrate? Weren't they the young Americans? Who cared that Prohibition was still going strong? Guys carried flasks tucked away in breast pockets, shiny jugs pulled out on the sly to splash gin into Cokes. Everyone was feeling good! There were no long faces around. Happy New Year, everyone!

Over there, in the middle of that mass of raucous tipsy people, Dolores and David showed off just how good they were at dancing each number that came along; they were tireless. Close by were Rosie and Ricky, kicking up a storm. Like everyone else, the four wore crazy little party hats that gave a cute touch to their new dresses and good-looking suits.

While Dolores and David danced their hearts out, they couldn't forget they were waiting for the Charleston contest, but they had to wait until after midnight. They grew more impatient as the hour got closer so they held each other close just to encourage one another.

"Relax, my Lola!" This was now his favorite name for her. "It's for sure. You're going to win."

"I can't help it. I don't want to be nervous, but my heart is beating real hard." She got even closer to David. "How do I look?"

"You're the most beautiful girl here. I love your hair. Here, have another sip." After she sipped, he said, "Here comes a slow one, let's dance so you can stay warmed up."

At last, Louie Armstrong interrupted his musicians to begin the countdown to twelve o'clock, with everyone belting out along with him. "Ten, nine, eight, seven, six, five, four, three, two, one!" And then, wild whistling and cheering broke out along with singing. "Should auld acquaintances be forgot..." Boozy off-key voices rang out in the middle of hugging and kissing, flasks openly pouring hooch while the din went on and on until it ran its course. Finally, the master of ceremonies stepped up to the microphone, but it took him at least three minutes to quiet down that almost out-of-control mob.

"Ladies and gentlemen, happy New Year!"

The crowd roared back, "Happy New Year!"

"It's time for our contest, and we're proud to announce we have thirteen signed-up contestants, so let's get down to it. Here are the rules:

"One, the contestants all come out dancing until one of our monitors taps the disqualified on her shoulder. That means better luck next time."

Vulgar raspberries blared through the air from a crowd anxious to get on with the contest.

"Two, Mr. Armstrong and his band will play the Charleston nonstop until the last remaining contestant is left.

"Three, The first prize will be awarded to that contestant."

Then the MC waved an envelope high over his head, proclaiming, "Here is the contract with MGM for the future celebrity. I regret to say that Mr. Thalberg won't be with us this evening to present the prize due to illness."

In drunken response, more raspberries, booing, and whistling broke out while the contestants, among them Dolores, made their way up to the stage. Lights on the dance floor dimmed, and then they were zoomed in on the girls who were nervously patting down hair, straightening spaghetti straps, and smoothing out creases on dresses. As for Dolores, the flashing spotlights highlighted the cobalt blue of her dress, making its sequin linings shimmer.

Without warning, the music came alive, and the dancing began. The Charleston's steps snapped into motion: heels clicking, legs flaring in opposite directions, elbows and arms flapping, knees knocking and gyrating, hips shifting, each step in sync with the rhythm of Louis Armstrong's uninhibited hot jazz. The dancers became a thunderous blur, but that's what the contest was all about.

In sync, the adoring crowd swayed, stomped and sang along, each one dancing without leaving their space on the dance floor. "Hey you! Yes You! Let's get flappin'. Feet in, feet out! Charleston, Charleston, everyone's wild about the Charleston!"

David was close to the stage, spellbound by Dolores's rhythmic steps, and his eyes suddenly filled with tears brought on by powerful feelings. *My destiny brought me here, to the most beautiful woman alive.* He, too, swayed to the rhythm of the music, and he did it without shifting an inch from where he stood, dazzled by Dolores's graceful natural movements.

Her arms were nimble, they didn't flap; instead, they moved and swayed to the beat of the music. Her body didn't mechanically bounce up and down; it undulated. Her shoulders weren't rigid; they rippled.

The dancing went on and on, but then fatigue set in; gyrations slowed, steps got sloppy, and soon, the shoulder tapping began. The number of contestants dwindled until there were only four left, then two, and finally the last one. Dolores Gómez kept on dancing although she had won, and that's when the crowded ballroom exploded into wild cheering because everyone knew from the beginning she had to be the one.

Dolores, moved by the deafening din, as well as by exhaustion, covered her face; she was crying, and along with those tears of utter joy was disbelief that her dream was coming true. She would soon be a movie star.

When the hoopla was over and Dolores was handed the gold-embossed envelop, she and David scurried out a side exit to walk on the pier, but the breeze sliding off the ocean was too cold. He slipped off his jacket and wrapped it around her shoulders, but it was still too cold to stay outdoors.

"Let's go to the car and wait there," said David. "Ricky and Rosie will come back sooner or later."

"Yes, it's too cold out here."

They sat in the back seat where he put his arm around her shoulders. Unexpectedly, Dolores put her head on his shoulder and kissed his neck; it was a soft, warm kiss. She had not done that before; she knew it was a daring thing to do, but she was overcome by a powerful compulsion to get close to David, closer than just holding hands, or being pressed against him on a crowded sidewalk. She needed more. She wanted to be one with him, wrapped around him. She wanted him inside her.

David responded with a long, intimate kiss but then sat very still, breathing hard, filled with a desire that grew as he looked at her, there in the darkened inside of Ricky's car, the light of the moon spilling from her hair onto her shoulders. She reached out and embraced him as no one had ever held him. Her arms were at once tender and ferocious, and all the time she kissed and kissed him. After a few moments, he edged off the seat and maneuvered himself onto the car's floorboard until he was kneeling in front of her. He unbuttoned his fly. She slipped off her panties, spread her knees, and surrendered.

Rocked by the frenzy of their lovemaking, the car pumped up, down, and then side to side. They forgot time and place. Neither did they care if they were seen, or whatever might happen afterward. Nothing mattered except the ecstasy that had hurled them into another world, into another time. When it was over, exhausted, they slumbered.

CHAPTER TWENTY-FIVE

A THIN ray of sunlight awoke Dolores. She blinked, looked around at the unfamiliar furniture, and then remembered she had slept over at Rosie's. She didn't move; instead, she closed her eyes. She needed to put her thoughts together.

David! She thought of him first. "Good night, my Lola," he whispered as he left her at the door of Rosie's room. "I'll see you tomorrow. Remember, I love you. I always will love you." She was awake now, and the sweetness of his breath still lingered, as did the light in his eyes.

Did it really happen?

A rush of new desire suddenly came over her as she remembered what they had done, right there in the car. Different thoughts crowded in, one pushing hard against the other. *Pain and pleasure at the same time! Is this what it means?* And the intense longing for more, to do it again and again. Dolores rolled her head on the pillow, wondering if she should be ashamed. She wasn't; neither did she have answers, only questions.

She thought of the contract with the studio, so she looked over to the table where she put the envelope just a few hours before. There it was, the envelope with gilded corners and MGM crest. It was real! She had not dreamed it. She danced her heart out, won the contest, and that, too, was real; no one could say it was made up. It was the beginning for her, and she smiled. Dolores stretched, got off the sofa, and headed for the bathroom. When she came out, she found Rosie, groggy and puffy-eyed, standing in the middle of the room.

"What's up, kiddo?"

"Good morning, Rosie! I have to go home. My mother will be worried. Can I borrow your coat and hat? It looks cold out there."

"What? How will you get there? It's New Year's Day, remember?"

"So?"

"So there're no buses. How do you expect to get all the way to Boyle Heights?"

"I'm sure there's a bus. I'm not the only one that has to get around. I'll make my way."

"What about David? He's bound to come around looking for you. What'll I say?"

"Tell him I'll be back this evening." Rosie made a face so Dolores went on. "C'mon, Rosie! I'll be back, I promise."

Mumbling, yawning, and still half-asleep, Rosie pulled her full-length coat and cloche hat out of the closet.

"Take it easy, kiddo. Don't get into any fights, okay? Remember, you're a winner."

Dolores made her way from Bunker Hill to downtown where she found a bus headed across the bridge to Sixth and Boyle. As she walked toward her house, she felt her stomach get funny; she was afraid of what they would say, and she didn't want to fight. She was too happy.

Her father was sitting on the porch, gazing at the street and passersby as Dolores walked up the steps. When she got near, she smiled and crouched to kneel by his lap, but he hardly reacted; he was neither surprised nor happy.

"Hello, Papa. Happy New Year!"

Something crossed her mind. She realized her father wasn't sick, or that his mind had left him; it was that he was profoundly sad, and this thought churned up the old feeling of guilt she had fought off for years.

After a while, Ignacio did notice his daughter's looks.

"You look different. I almost didn't recognize you."

"I cut my hair. Do you like it?"

He didn't answer; instead, he told her to join the others. "They're enjoying their day off."

Dolores straightened up and made her way through the front door toward the sound of jabbering voices coming from the kitchen. She stood for a moment, listening to their laughter mixed in with the clink of dishes, forks, and glasses; she breathed in the delicious aroma of what her mother was putting together. But she was getting even more nervous now that she was close to facing them, so she took a deep breath and walked into the kitchen.

It was as if the Santa Ana wind had blown the roof off the house when Dolores walked into the kitchen. The shock wasn't so much because she was unexpected, which she was; it was that she was transformed. Altagracia stared at her wide-eyed, as did Pilar and Sebastián. Even Valeria, sitting in her high chair, sensed something special was happening; and Cele, a ladle held in mid-air, froze. Only Héctor was unfazed.

Dolores forgot she had changed her appearance overnight. Her hair, now short and wavy, was tucked under the dark-blue velveteen cloche hat that emphasized the heavy makeup on her eyes and lips; flirty spit curls were pasted on each cheek. She didn't think of how the full-length coat, also dark blue, made her look taller and slimmer. Its fur collar made her another sort of person, so did the purse dangling from her arm and the high-heeled, strapped, patent leather shoes. And the family had as yet to get a glimpse of her new flapper dress.

"I knew it! I told you she's gone crazy!"

That was Altagracia letting out her old singsong, but no one else said anything. They were tongue-tied, speechless, struck dumb, and there wasn't a sound after Altagracia's gushing. It was Cele who recovered first. She quietly put down the spoon, made her way to her daughter, and took her in her arms. Dolores responded by eagerly wrapping her arms around her mother.

"Come in, Dolores. You're just on time. I made your favorite chicken."

Without saying anymore, Cele pulled a chair away from a corner, gently moved Héctor to make room at the table, and asked her if she wanted something to drink before dinner. Dolores took off her coat and hat, sat down, and after a minute or two, the chatter took off again. In a while, Sebastián wiped his mouth and looked at Dolores; his voice was cold.

"Where were you last night?"

All eyes turned to look at her. It was a question on everyone's mind, but since Dolores had expected something like this, she kept calm.

"At a dance. Where were you?"

"I was here, with my family, where else?" He took a mouthful and, again, wiped his mouth. "I'm getting married, Dolores."

This time, Sebastián did take her by surprise. She knew—they all knew—he had a relationship by letter with someone in their old town, but no one expected the connection to go anywhere. Dolores, trying not to show her surprise, put down her fork.

"Who are you marrying?"

"Ofelia Canales. You went to school with her."

"I don't remember her." She wrinkled her brow, trying to put a face on the name. "Where did she live?"

"Close to where we lived." Sebastián sat up even straighter as he described the girl he intended to marry. "She's beautiful, but more important, she's a good girl."

Dolores caught his meaning but decided not to react. She knew her brother thought less of her because of her new ways, and especially because she did what she wanted.

"Yeah! And she's not crazy like some other people we know."

Altagracia couldn't help herself. Sebastián grinned, but Cele put a stop to it right away.

"That's enough, Altagracia. Pass the rice!"

Sebastián had more to say. "I'm leaving next week to marry her, and she's coming back to live here with us." He glared at Dolores, expecting her to say something, but she didn't respond. She knew he wanted to talk more about his plans, but she decided not to give him the satisfaction, so she went on eating without saying anymore.

After they finished dinner, Cele took Dolores by the elbow and headed for the front room, but not before turning to her children. "Wash the dishes, and get everything ready for breakfast tomorrow. Héctor, watch Valeria! Come with me, Dolores."

Dolores knew the time had come for the truth to come out, and although she was shaky, she was relieved; it was what she wanted. Her mother wasn't a woman who swallowed lies, so why even try?

The front room was large but cozy. It had a big window facing the grassy front yard; it was at this window that Cele often sat when she needed to think. As she and Dolores walked into the room, the sun was beginning to dip; its late-afternoon light brought a melancholy feeling to the room that washed over mother and daughter. They sat side by side on the sofa and began their conversation with small talk, speaking in low soft tones.

But then, Dolores, anxious to let her mother know she had accomplished something special, moved on from the chitchat and took the MGM envelope from her purse.

"Look, Mama, see what a good thing has happened to me."

She pulled the sheet of paper from the envelope and put it in Cele's hands. Her mother took the paper, smoothed it out, but then looked up at Dolores.

"Dolores, you know I don't read this language. What does it say?"

"I forgot!" She took the paper from her mother's hands. "It says I've been given a job with a Hollywood studio beginning next week."

"Work? Doing what?"

"I'm not sure yet, Mama, but it will put me where I can begin training to be an actress."

After a moment's pause, Cele asked, "Is that what you want to be?"

It was part of Cele's nature that whatever thought crossed her mind was immediately reflected on her face; now she was showing surprise and disbelief, along with a lot of doubt. Dolores understood the look right away, and she didn't like it. She had expected a burst of joy, even pride, in her accomplishment.

"How did you get it?"

Dolores hesitated, she was losing confidence fast, but she had to let her mother know what it was all about.

"I won a dance contest."

"A dance contest! Where? When?"

"Last night at a ballroom in Santa Monica."

"This must be a joke. You don't believe it, do you?"

Dolores's shakiness turned to irritation, and now she was confused as well. "It's not a joke! It's for real! This is how all the movie stars get started. It has to be done from the bottom up."

Cele wagged her head in frustration. "Dolores, you're not thinking clearly. You're too intelligent to believe this lie. Besides, only one in a million reaches such heights."

Stung, Dolores reacted, "Lie! How can you say it's a lie?" Her voice became shrill. "Mama, studios don't lie! It was the promised prize, and I won it. No one can deny it! You should have heard the applause and cheering!"

Cele caught her daughter's frustration and saw she was nearly in tears, so she mellowed and stayed quiet. Meanwhile, Dolores fidgeted with the hem of her dress.

"I can see you're taking this whole thing seriously." At last, Cele spoke. "Fine! I, too, will believe it. The only thing I ask is that you not give up your work at the restaurant until you get a good feeling for what this new job will give you. Do you think this is a good idea?"

Cele's calm as well as her decision to believe the studio job was real, relieved Dolores's distress. Besides, her mother's advice made sense; she, too, had already decided not to give up her job at the diner.

"Thank you, Mama. I'm happy you see it this way. Nothing will change, except I will live with my friend starting tonight. She lives closer to Hollywood, and it's easier for me to go from one job to the other from her place."

Cele's eyes suddenly turned darker, sharper. Dolores had tried to slip in this last part as casually as possible, knowing it was the most important, but it didn't fool her mother. Those words, uttered by Dolores in such a matter-of-fact way, hit Cele hard. They alarmed her more than knowing about the dance contest and its prize; they worried her even more than her daughter's changed image and different clothes.

What Cele heard was that Dolores was leaving her family home to live among strangers, people with a different way of thinking and behaving. Cele's worst fears, the ones she harbored from the beginning of their journey away from their homeland, were coming true. This realization hit her hard, and she retreated into a brooding silence while Esperanza's face appeared to her as if out of a mist. *Am I going to lose this second daughter as well? And what of Pilar and Altagracia? Will they also become like Dolores?*

"Mama, did you hear what I said?"

"Yes, I heard every word."

Cele looked into her daughter's eyes, and with that mysterious power of discernment Cele possessed, she bluntly asked, "There's something else you need to tell me, isn't there?"

Unnerved, Dolores hesitated, trying to think of what to answer. She had to think of something, anything, yet it couldn't be about David and what happened in the back seat of the car. She stuttered, trying to put words together, but Cele abruptly cut her off.

"Are you going to live with your girlfriend, or with a man?"

"Mama! What are you thinking? I'm going to live with Rosie. She works at the restaurant with me."

"Is there a man, Dolores?"

It was no use! Dolores closed her eyes, and she let her mouth say what it had to say.

"Yes, there's a boy."

"How old is he?"

"Twenty-four."

"He is not a boy! He's a man! And you're a woman now, aren't you?"

Her words sounded like a question, but it wasn't a question. Cele was making a statement.

"Mama, I'm nineteen."

"I know your age. I'm saying you're a woman now. Am I right?"

Dolores knew what her mother meant, but she didn't answer right away. Instead she took a deep breath before saying, "Yes."

And that ended the conversation between Dolores and her mother in that melancholy front room. No more was said except for the stupid little things people say after they've emptied a heavy heart.

"You need to take some of your things, don't you?"

"Yes, Mama."

Cele went to the kitchen and returned with a couple of brown paper shopping bags. Dolores went to her room, filled the bags with underwear, clothes, and other things. When she walked out onto the porch, she found her mother sitting next to Ignacio, so Dolores stood quietly looking at the two people she loved so much.

"Mama, Papa, his name is David Katagian, and he wants to meet all of you. Can I bring him tomorrow?"

"Yes," said Cele. "You can invite him to stay for dinner, if you want."

Dolores kissed them, walked down the porch's short flight of steps, and onto the street toward the bus stop.

Afterward, Cele spent the night sleepless, thinking of Dolores; maybe she had been too harsh with her daughter. She didn't want to lose her; what she wanted was her happiness. Cele's head was a whirl of questions touched off by worry. Had she not always feared that this very thing might happen? Wasn't the breakup of her family one of her terrors? Now Dolores was slipping through her fingers, but Cele didn't know when or how it started. Had she been careless or stupid in her care of Dolores? Had she missed the signs? Was it her fault?

The night crept by; nothing moved or made a sound, and Cele tossed restlessly in her place next to Ignacio, who was so still he might have been dead. Once, she even put her face close to his nose to assure that he was breathing.

She thought mostly of the next day's meeting with Dolores's friend, knowing their first encounter would be a turning point. She knew that Sebastián would be looking to her for guidance, for the way to deal with the stranger, so her words had to be the right ones. They had to let Sebastián know she was ready to support Dolores despite what the family considered forbidden or indecent. If she said it the right way, she was certain Sebastián and the others would follow her lead.

When these thoughts became clear to Cele, she relaxed knowing that what was in her heart would spill out when she met with Dolores and the man. She wanted tomorrow to turn out right, that it pave the way for Dolores to be happy, to be free. This good intention, Cele knew, would come out of her mouth, and into her family's ears.

She closed her eyes, desperately wanting to fall asleep, but something else nagged at her: No matter how much she tried, Cele couldn't rid herself of thinking that what the stranger was really doing was stealing Dolores away from her family, and this thought filled her with a terrible conflict. *If down deep I think of him as a thief, how can I wish them well?*

She wanted to like the so-called David, or whatever his name was, but she found herself dangerously on the verge of hating him even before knowing him. She finally fell asleep during the last hours of the night, but when she awoke the next morning, she was grumpy and depressed.

CHAPTER TWENTY-SIX

THEY SAT thigh-to-thigh on the bus heading for her family's home. The bus was packed, and overflow passengers crowded into the middle aisle, hanging on to the upper rail, struggling to keep their balance each time the vehicle started, stopped, or made a sharp turn. The bus was filled with the noise of chatting people, squawking kids, and the hum of the vehicle's engine. When David and Dolores spoke to each other, they had to put their heads close, lips to ear, but they didn't mind it. They liked the closeness.

"I hope they like me," he said this as he slipped his arm through hers. "I speak a little Spanish, but not much."

"I know they'll like you," she answered. "And except for Mama and Papa, the rest speak English, like I do."

"It's okay. I can hold a conversation in Spanish, if it's short." And then he smiled and asked, "I'm a little nervous, aren't you?"

"Just a little. It's Sebastián that worries me."

"How come?"

"Well, since my father stopped being the boss, my brother, along with my mother, has taken over. And he can be really bossy."

"What's the matter with your father?"

"It's hard to explain. A lot happened to make him sad, or something like that. He's just not himself. Leaving Mexico was really tough for him."

David gazed through the window at the commotion going on outside. "Leaving one's land is hard, Dolores. I know what it feels like." He paused but then said, "It's the same with us."

"What is?"

"That the oldest brother takes the place of the father. It would be the same with my family except everybody was killed."

She looked at him and felt of pity, but at the same time, she remembered the chaos her own family had left behind.

"David, there's something else I want to talk about before we get to the house." She stopped for a few moments. "My other brother, Héctor, was injured so bad he's not right up here." She pointed at her head. "He doesn't act like the rest of us."

David was surprised. He thought she had told him everything about her family the first night.

"How was he injured?"

"He was beat up. Nearly killed. He's lucky to be alive."

"When did it happen?"

"We still lived in Kingman where he got involved with some bad guys."

"And they beat him up? Why?"

Dolores was getting uncomfortable; she didn't want to tell David more. It was shameful, but now, she had gone too far to stop.

"Héctor fooled around with a girl, and her brothers got even. They thought they had killed him."

"For being with their sister? Was that all?"

"No! There was more to it!" Her voice was showing exasperation. "He made her pregnant, and that really pissed off those guys, so they beat the shit out of him." Dolores folded her arms on her chest to show there wasn't more to the story, but then added, "He didn't die, but he's a vegetable now."

The bus's movement was slow. Traffic was heavy, and the vehicle's constant stop and go made talking difficult.

"That's hard on a family, Lola!"

David kept quiet for a while wondering why Dolores hadn't told about her brother in the beginning.

"Why didn't you mention this before?"

"Ashamed, I guess."

"What happened to the kid?"

"We kept her. Valeria lives with us. She's a cute kid."

His head rocked along with the bus's swaying. "Lola, I'm going to like Héctor. Maybe I can help him."

She looked at him, surprise stamped on her face, but then, in a minute, she said, "Yes. I think you would be good for him. We've never really done anything except care for him. No doctors or anything like that. He seems pretty alone, isolated, if you know what I mean." Then she added, "My father is really quiet too. Don't think it's because of you. He's that way all the time." She looked out the window and said, "Next stop is ours."

Dolores and David didn't walk right into the house but knocked on the screen door and waited. In a minute, footsteps sounded, and the front door opened. It was Pilar, so nervous she didn't know what to do or say.

"Hi, Dolores."

"Unlatch the door, Pilar!"

"Okay. Okay."

Dolores had expected to show David to the kitchen where it was usual for the family to get together, but she saw right away they were sitting in the front room. Ignacio, Cele, and Pilar, with Valeria on her lap, sat on the couch; and Altagracia was sitting on a stool by Héctor. Only Sebastián was on his feet, arms crossed on his chest, and he was leaning against the wall, making Dolores think he was in a hostile mood, and that things were not going to be okay.

Still standing in the doorway, she said, "Hello, everyone." Her voice was thin and shaky, but then she cleared her throat and tried again, her nervousness still obvious. "This is my friend, David Katagian."

No one said anything, much less smiled; they stared at Dolores and David as if they had been intruders. David, however, didn't leave it all to Dolores. He stood next to her and greeted them with his usual strong but gentle voice.

"Hello. I'm David Katagian, and I'm glad to be here to meet you."

He sensed the hostility in the room, but he had walked into that house with one intention on his mind: to show them how much he loved and respected Dolores, and that he wanted to be a friend. This intent gave him courage, although he had to admit he felt seriously intimidated.

Sebastián was the first to speak, but he did it, looking only at his sister, obviously ignoring David.

"Where's this guy from, Dolores?"

David didn't shy away from the slight; he spoke up before Dolores opened her mouth.

"I'm from Armenia, but now I live here in Los Angeles."

"I wasn't talking to you, Pal! I was talking to my sister."

It wasn't a good beginning. Sebastián was no longer leaning against the wall but stood, feet planted apart, with his fists shoved deep into his trouser pockets. The rest of the family participated in their own way. Ignacio, as if in a trance, stared wide-eyed at the floor, Pilar and Altagracia's faces swiveled to stare at whomever was speaking. Héctor sat, head bent low, eyes closed. For her part, Cele sat up straight, eyes focused, but she was as yet silent.

By now, Dolores had recovered her voice. "Why are you being so rude, Sebastián? We're here because we want to be friends." Then, looking at her mother and father, she said, "Because we want to honor you, Mama and Papa."

Cele at last spoke up, and although she did so in Spanish, David understood her.

"Let's calm down! Dolores, your friend is welcomed, but he must understand that we need time to get used to your new way of living."

This wasn't a good beginning for Cele either, especially since it wasn't what she had intended to say.

"What do you mean, Mama?"

"Well, living away from us is what I mean. You know it's not customary for decent girls to live away from home. Not unless they have something to be ashamed of."

The moment Cele heard her own words, she regretted them. But now, loose and irretrievable, those words sped straight to Sebastián.

Incensed by what her mother was implying, Dolores half turned around, ready to bolt out of the house, but she didn't because David held her back. When he spoke, his voice had not lost its gentle tone, but it was on the edge.

"Your daughter, señora, hasn't done anything indecent." Although he spoke in Spanish with a heavy accent, they all understood. "If she needs to live with her friend, it's only because it's closer to her work. What's indecent about that?"

"You don't get to speak to my mother!" Sebastián yelled out. "If you were a real man, you wouldn't let my sister leave her family to do indecent things."

At this point, David's restraints collapsed; his anger flared. "Come outside to see what kind of a man I am." His voice was loud, menacing; even his stance changed, and his posture became hostile.

Sebastián, a head taller than David, sneered, "Ha! I don't fight with midgets."

Goaded beyond what he could bear, David sprang. At the same time, Pilar, clutching Valeria, leaped from the couch and ran out of the room. Altagracia did the same thing just as Héctor let out a nerve-shattering scream, a half moan, half shriek so jarring it compelled Sebastián, who was about to lunge at David, to stop in his tracks. Héctor's terrible wail also triggered Ignacio out of his trance. As tall as his son, and still strong, he leaped out of his seat, spread his stiffened arms, palms held up like shields, one pointed at Sebastián, the other at David.

"Stop! Back off! This is still my home!" Sebastián and David retreated. "Dolores, you and your friend should leave. We can do this a better way at another time."

Dolores grabbed David's hand, and together they stumbled away, both deeply shaken. Dolores, with her face smeared with tears of rage, regretted having brought David to face such an ordeal. It was also a surprise for her to have seen David change from the gentle person she was getting to love into someone capable of murder. Without a word, they made their way back to the bus stop.

The ride back to Rosie's place happened in stunned silence. When Dolores and David arrived, instead of going into her place to face Rosie, they decided to walk up to the top of the hill where they found a secluded cluster of overgrown palm trees. David took off his overcoat, spread it on the ground, and they sat there quietly, looking up at the shimmering stars. Neither spoke. They were still in the grip of the terrible encounter they experienced with her family.

David was on edge, still enraged and trying to erase the image of the room packed with angry people he didn't know. Dolores was fighting back tears of humiliation, trying to deal with her mother's words that made her feel like trash.

"David, are you mad at me?" Dolores finally broke the ice.

"Why should I be mad at you? You didn't do anything wrong."

"I'm ashamed!"

"Don't be. It had to happen. I'm the one who should be ashamed."

"Why?"

"I lost control. It doesn't happen too much, but I have to say your brother knows how to start a fight."

"He learned to do it when he was little."

They retreated back into silence while the inner turmoil assaulting them gradually lessened. David's heartbeat was almost normal now; and Dolores, too, had pushed back on her tears.

"Lola, we have to think that it can't be so bad. You'll see. Your family will think it over and change their minds. Things will be better."

She looked at him, and even in the gloom, she made out how sincere David felt. She saw that he really thought there was hope for them to be accepted by her family.

"I don't care if they change their minds. I never want to see them again."

"Don't say that!"

"Why not? It's what I mean."

"You might regret it later on."

"David, what should we do?"

"For now, we should think of our life together."

Dolores didn't say anything. Then they moved closer; it was a chilly night, and they craved each other's warmth. Still quiet, she caressed his cheek, giving David such indescribable joy he moved even closer to kiss her. Their tongues touched, held, and when they let go, more caresses and sighs followed until the intensity of their passion overcame them, and they surrendered to it. In the silence of that dark oasis, they took off their clothes, and one loving touch followed the other until he was inside her.

David and Dolores at last felt safe after so much bitterness. They knew they were protected by starlight and gentle palm shadows, even as the earth beneath their naked bodied shook, and so they loved each other again, and yet again, until exhaustion overcame them. Then they drifted. After a while, David put his arm under her head and pulled his coat to cover them. When he spoke, his voice was husky, still in the thrall of lovemaking.

"Look, Lola, how the lights shine as far as you can see."

She opened her eyes to look down at the busiest streets of downtown Los Angeles, still glimmering with leftover holiday lights. Then she gazed toward the river to look at its bridges fringed by tall light posts. The air was clear that crisp January night, so she could see even beyond those lights all the way to a thick blur on the eastern horizon.

"What's that dark spot way out there?"

"Mountains."

"I want to live there. Right now!"

Dolores moved her face closer to his; she wanted to feel his breath. David put his nose against her cheek so he, too, could breathe in her fragrance.

"One day soon, my Lola, I'm going to build you a palace at the foot of those mountains. It will have floors made of blue and gold tiles, countless arches and pillars, and a big pool with a fountain in the middle. The ceilings of that mansion will be painted with cherubs and archangels, each with a golden trumpet to ring out with music for you."

"*Dios mío!* Your mansion sounds more like a church than our house. Remember we're not rich, at least not yet." She laughed. "Wait until I become a famous movie star, then we'll have that mansion, not in the mountains but in Beverly Hills. At any rate, I thought you said all you wanted was a little house for our kids and me. Now it's a mansion."

David didn't pay attention. Instead, he dreamed on because he felt his bitterness and anger fading away with each word.

"You'll be as glorious as the queen of Sheba when she entered Jerusalem at the head of a train of camels covered in rich tapestries and silver harnesses."

"David, that's beautiful. Your dreams are like a Rudolf Valentino movie."

"Yeah, a movie that really happened a long time ago."

Then they kept quiet again. They didn't fool themselves; they knew they were daydreaming, and that their reality was too harsh to even come close to what they were imagining. On the other hand, Dolores and David were young, in love, and optimistic. Hadn't they managed to put behind them the ugliness they had just experienced? They had, and they were grateful. After their lovemaking and daydreaming, they felt cleansed; and for that, too, they were thankful, but now it was time to make plans that were reachable.

"When is your appointment at the studio?" Even his voice sounded different.

"Next Friday."

"I'll borrow Ricky's car to drive you."

"Thanks!"

"Then we'll look for a place of our own." When Dolores raised her eyebrows, he went on. "You can't move in where I live, and I can't move in with you and Rosie. We need our own place."

Surprised, Dolores looked at David for a few moments, wondering if he was joking.

"Are you serious?"

"Yes!"

"But we're not married."

"Well then, let's go ahead and marry."

"I don't want to marry."

"You don't want to be with me?"

"I didn't say that. I just don't want to marry. Not yet, not until I become an actress."

David again flashed his broad smile. "Can't we live together in the meantime?"

"No! It's a sin."

He propped himself up on an elbow and toyed with something on the ground.

"I remember my mother used to talk a lot about sin when I was a boy. Back then, it meant not eating one's food because others in the world were starving. Later on, sin meant something more serious. It meant killing your enemy."

Dolores frowned, unsure she was following. "Living together before getting married is a sin, but it's not like murder."

Smiling, he answered, "You mean it's a little sin."

"No, I mean it's a smaller sin."

He grinned again. "Well then, let's live together in a smaller sin."

"You're laughing at me!"

"No! I'm not laughing at you. What I'm saying is that I do see a difference, but honestly, Lola, how can what you and I feel for each other be bad? That's all I'm saying. I want to marry you, but you want to wait. Okay! I can see why you want to wait. But in the meantime, we can't live apart. Do you know what I mean?"

Dolores took time to answer, all the while gazing at the twinkling carpet of lights spread out beneath them. Finally, she spoke up. "Yes. I understand what you're saying. And yes, I want to live with you." She kept quiet, thinking before she went on. "Although what we're going to do is really what my mother and brother accused me of doing. I guess they were right. I am doing something indecent."

"Indecent?" David sat up the better to peer into her face. "What's indecent about living together? Can loving one another like we do be something to be ashamed of? No, it isn't! Not to me!"

"No, I'm not ashamed either."

After this, Dolores and David had sex again, but in the recesses of their minds, there still lingered a quiet, nagging anxiety.

CHAPTER TWENTY-SEVEN

CELE GOT to her feet and stood for a while on the back porch, looking out over rooftops and light posts. Her movements were slow, listless, but she forced herself to go back into the house to look for Sebastián. She searched every room, but she found only sleeping people. It wasn't until she went into the front room that she found him slumped on the sofa staring out the window; he, too, was drained. She sat next to him.

He mumbled, "What have we done, Mama?"

"We've broken something beautiful."

Her words worked like a prod on him, and he turned in the seat so suddenly it made her flinch.

"Don't say that! It's my sister who's done something wrong!"

"Has she?"

Sebastián, his nerves still raw from the clash with David, and now confused by his mother's unexpected turnaround, repeated what he thought.

"Yes! She *has* done something wrong." He hit his knee with a clenched fist. "Or do you imagine that at this very minute she's not fornicating with that intruder?"

His words hit Cele hard; they hurt so much she winced.

"When did you become so vulgar?"

"Vulgar? Mama, isn't it Dolores who is vulgar? Yes or no?"

Cele felt unfairly pressed by her son, so she answered with as much force, "I won't judge her."

"You should judge her!"

"Why?"

"Because what she's doing is wrong!"

"How do I know if what she's doing is wrong?"

Baffled, Sebastián slouched back and stared at her, obviously not knowing what to think. "Mama, that's not what you said a while ago." His voice was husky, maybe on the verge of tears.

"I know, I know! But what I said wasn't in my heart, and I can't explain why I said it. What I do know is that I'll regret those words for the rest of my life."

Sebastián was now so upset he got to his feet to pace back and forth.

"Listen to what you're saying! Dolores will live with that man, without your and Papa's blessing, much less that of a priest. That's a sin! Doesn't that mean something to you?"

"How can you be so sure? She said she was leaving because of her work because living with her friend is closer to where she works. Why shouldn't we believe her?"

"Oh, God, Mama! You believe that shit?"

"Watch your words!" Cele paused and then added, "Yes, I believe her!"

"I don't!"

"I know, Sebastián, but I'm her mother, and I know her heart is pure."

Sebastián felt the room spinning; he was having a hard time with his mother's change of heart.

"Haven't you taught us the difference between wrong and right?" He hovered over Cele. "Dolores, just as much as Pilar, Altagracia, me—we were all taught by you. Now you're saying what she's doing isn't a sin?"

"I'm saying I'm not going to judge her."

Sebastián sat down again, now closer to Cele. He took her hands in his as his expression changed from exasperation to uncertainty.

"I don't understand what you mean. I want to, but I can't. I'm so mad at Dolores for so much. I want to punish her for tearing us apart, for acting like a spoiled kid, for stepping all over what we think is important."

"Ay! Sebastián! Now it's your turn to listen to your own words. What exactly has Dolores done to tear us apart, as you say? Isn't it you? Isn't it me, especially, that's done that much? Honestly, when I stop crying,

I'm going to see that this was all a ridiculous mistake. I'm going to see everything clearly, and that it's not the end of the world."

"Christ, Mama! You're driving me crazy! First you say this, and then you say another thing! I don't know what you really think, and it's killing me!"

"What do you want me to say?" Now it was Cele's voice that was rising, more angry than sad. "Do you want me to say I'll throw her out if ever she returns? Or maybe you want me to put a curse on her, like mothers do in our families." She paused. "I'm not going to do that, Sebastián." Her voice dropped to a murmur. "Not now, not ever!"

Sebastián glared at Cele then said, "What will you say to Ofelia when she returns as my wife? Won't you be ashamed to tell of Dolores?"

"No, I won't be ashamed because I have nothing to be ashamed of, and I hope your wife will understand."

On the edge of disgust, Sebastián got to his feet; he had nothing more to say. As he was turning to leave the room, Cele's words stopped him.

"I want you to look for Dolores."

"What?"

"Yes, find her, and tell her we want her back."

Hardly believing what he was hearing, Sebastián shot back, "I don't know where to look for her—not where she sleeps or even where she works. Do you?"

Dismayed, Cele looked at her son.

"No, I don't."

"Do you know the name of the place where she works?"

"No."

"Do you know of a friend, or somebody that could help me find her?"

"Dolores spoke of someone called Rosie."

"Rosie? What's her last name? I would need that much to even begin looking her up."

Cele bit her lip and frowned. "I don't remember your sister mentioning a last name."

"Well, what good is a first name? Los Angeles is a big city. It's bigger than any place we've ever lived in. I can't just go to any street corner and start asking, 'Do you know where I can find Rosie?'"

Her son's sarcasm rankled Cele although she knew he was right. "You can at least try." Her voice was thin and filled with frustration.

Cele heard herself losing control as exasperation, even desperation, overcame her. She heard Sebastián's questions, and because she couldn't answer any of them, she feared that maybe Dolores, like Esperanza, would be swallowed up by an unknown street, a restaurant, a room, all of them in plain sight yet hidden simply because she didn't know where to look, and that she, Cele, would again end up powerless to find her daughter.

Defeated, she slumped back on the sofa, but her distress, and the strong tie that bound Sebastián to her since before he could remember, deeply moved him. He scrambled to her side.

"Listen to me, Mama!" His voice was now warm, understanding. "You know I'll be leaving to get married this week, but when I return with Ofelia, you and I will look for Dolores, and find her. I promise!"

Cele couldn't speak anymore, so she nodded, took his hands in hers, and gently patted them. "I'll wait."

He kissed her forehead and murmured, "Good night, Mama," and left the room.

Drained and exhausted by the day's happenings, Cele stayed for a few minutes more until she regained some strength. She remembered there were lights to be turned off, as well as doors and windows that should be shut for the night; she took hold of the sofa's armrest and used it to get on her feet. Once upright, she rubbed her back and slowly made her way to finish her last chores of the day.

"I'll wait," she said under her breath, not once but over and again.

CHAPTER TWENTY-EIGHT

THE EARLY days of 1929 gave way to the dry Santa Ana winds of summer and year's end. In the meantime, it seemed that the world hung in suspense, as if waiting. Nothing was for certain. On the other hand, what people knew for sure was that there was no need to wait for the good times to roll; every day was a party. No one waited for a job, they were everywhere, and most people had money stashed away in the bank.

Cele, however, waited during those last months of 1929, so when Sebastián returned with his wife, they began their search for Dolores. They scoured busy streets, asking at restaurants, shops, factories; they looked her up at boarding houses and even might-be neighbors and laundry workers, all the time asking, even showing Dolores's picture, but it was no use. It was as if she had evaporated, and so Cele was left empty-handed with nothing else to do but wait and hope for the return of her daughter.

As Cele waited, on a certain August evening, not that far from her, David stood looking at the duplex he and Dolores had just rented. It was a furnished place on Vignes Street near the train station and close to the Olympic Auditorium where he was now working. He had left the gym when the auditorium offered him a better job, even though he did it hoping that Shorty wouldn't mind. He didn't. In fact, he was happy for David.

He sighed as he sat on the sofa, grateful that destiny had put him on the path that led to the woman he loved above all things as well as to a new life that he liked. Even his new job was good. Boxing and wrestling matches were big in Los Angeles, and he was in the middle of the action since he was in charge of the promotion and publicity of those events.

David liked the job mostly because he was expected to show up in a suit and tie and to be in charge. The job worked well with his personality, and it also meant more money.

As he stood in his new home's front room, he took a minute to look out the window at the houses along the block; he liked the neighborhood. They were frame houses of different sizes, neat, all of them with fresh coats of paint. On the other hand, he was preoccupied by something else. He often thought about the awful clash with the Gómez family; their angry faces still haunted him despite his efforts to erase them. The brother, David thought, was the worst; but the mother's eyes were seared into his mind as well.

He took a deep breath, and to distract himself from that memory, he thought of Zepyur—he often did—wishing she could see him now. *And it's just the beginning, Old One!* He spoke to her, too, so he smiled as he took a pack of Lucky Strikes from his shirt pocket. He had recently taken up smoking, mostly because it let him blend in with his friends. He lit up.

After the joy of living with Dolores, there were two things that made David happier: opening a savings account at the bank and buying a Model T Ford. It was a used one, but it was a good deal. The vehicle gave him a chance to learn what made a car run, and he discovered that he was intrigued by mechanics. His mind then moved on to think of his next step: Buy a car shop to give him more money than his job and then a house so he and Dolores could start their family.

But it was the bank account that gave him the most satisfaction because he was convinced it was proof that he was a real American. He always carried the deposit booklet tucked into his wallet, often taking time to pull it out and examine his deposits. It was thrilling for him just to look at the columns of zeros add up; it made him feel secure and grateful for what he was putting together.

There was a curious side to David, however; something that compelled him to put at least some of his money aside in a drawer and not put it all in the bank. Maybe it was an unconscious distrust of banks that made him squirrel away at least some of his cash. Otherwise, he didn't mind standing in line to deposit most of his money every payday; it made him feel good watching the cashier add numbers to the deposit column.

The cashier always said, "Good going, Mr. Katagian! See you next Friday!"

And he would answer, "Thanks! See you then."

David sighed again, took a long drag, slowly exhaled, and watched the smoky ring drift toward the ceiling. It was evening, and he was waiting for Dolores to return from her routine at the studio. He planned on inviting her out to dinner to celebrate their anniversary. Which one? He wasn't sure how long since he and Dolores had been together, but what difference did it make? It had to be the anniversary of something or another.

In the meantime, he would just relax, sit back to enjoy his new place, and think of how good life was for him and Dolores. They had good money now, just like everyone else, and they used it on good-looking clothes and restaurants. Both liked to get dressed up to go out dancing on the weekends just as much as they enjoyed canoeing most Sundays on the Echo Park lake. Dolores's favorite way to pass a day was to spend it at the Long Beach Pike. They did it all and still had extra money to put aside in the bank.

David pulled away from those thoughts to think of Dolores's family again, and that there had not been any contact since that terrible day in January. This troubled him since he hoped something would have happened by now to get them together, but Dolores was against their being the ones to take a first step.

He scratched his chin, thinking of how he had got to know something new about her every day. One of those things was that she hung on to a grudge; it wasn't easy for her to forgive and forget. The other side of Dolores he got to know was her strange moodiness. Sometimes she was so cheerful; nothing could dim that high feeling in her, but then, that same happiness could swing suddenly into moroseness so deep and solid it frightened him.

These thoughts moved on to memories of his family: his brother and sister, grandmother and father, but especially his mother. Funny! It had been a long time since their faces had appeared out of his misty past, so now, eyes half-closed, he let those images float around him. He wondered what they would look like now if the Turks had not assassinated them. Would the old ones be wrinkled and stooped? he wondered. For sure, his sister would be a beauty. Would his brother be taller than him, more muscular? For sure, he wouldn't be more handsome! David chuckled and went on imagining what could never happen.

What would his loved ones think of their boy now that he was transplanted to this land so far from Old Armenia? Would they be astounded that little David had survived the vileness of the orphanage? What would they think of the boy who made his way across continents alongside a wizened old woman and who became the apprentice of a Jewish mentor? What would they think of that same boy who became a man when he murdered a Turk?

David shuddered thinking of that part of his life's story. He distractedly ran his fingers through his hair, thinking he would give anything to bring back those loved ones if only for a few moments. But it was impossible, so he turned to thinking of his life as it was now. He glanced at his wristwatch, thinking that Dolores should get there at any minute.

He wanted to have a nice time with Dolores that evening; it troubled him they had been bickering so much lately. Was it his fault? Maybe. It was hard to tell. At times he thought it was that she was exasperated by not moving up the ladder of success sooner, but as he reminded her, *"You're in the middle of it. It's only a matter of time."* But Dolores was impatient; she wanted to go up fast, and do it fast.

For his part, David wanted her to become a star or whatever she dreamed, although he had serious doubts, not because she wasn't beautiful enough or talented enough; she was that much, and more, he was convinced. In fact, she was more beautiful than most of those famous fake-looking women everyone saw in the movies.

Yet he had misgivings, but he didn't know why. Maybe it was because the odds against making it were so great for anyone in that business, but he learned to keep his thoughts to himself after the one time he made the mistake of letting his doubts slip out.

When Dolores heard him tell her that maybe she should try something else, she blew up so badly it scared him, and what was worse, she didn't talk to him for a week afterward. David learned that lesson fast; but he saw, too, that things weren't bad after they quarreled: They ended up each time making love, and this was worth it all, he thought.

He glanced at his watch again. *Where is she?*

At that moment, Dolores was on the bus heading home from a day at the studio, exhausted but thrilled. She had worked all day rehearsing on a chorus line, and although she loved the excitement, it was hard work, and she was relieved to hear, "Okay, girls! Wrap it up!" The director shouted out what everyone was waiting to hear, and in a second, there was the racket of dance shoes making a beeline for the off-stage doorway.

"Gómez, hang on!"

When Dolores heard her name shouted out above the din of chattering, giggling chorus girls, she got a funny feeling in her stomach. She patted her hair, looked to see that her tights were okay, and then she walked over to the director who was sitting at the piano.

"Well, kid, I've got good news for you."

Her stomach tightened up again, this time, for a different reason.

"The studio is coming out this year with a big—I mean a really big—production. Its title right now is 'Gold Diggers of Broadway' and it's going to feature big names, so many I won't even begin to name them. We need good hoofers for most of the scenes, and they have to not only be good dancers, they have to be knockouts too. We've chosen a few already, and you're one of them."

Dolores's face must have paled or reddened or something because the director asked, "You all right, Dodo?" He called her by the nickname the girls now used for her.

"Yeah! Wally! I'm fine. I'm just really surprised."

"Surprised? Is that all?"

"Oh, yeah! Very surprised! I think I'm going to faint it feels so good!"

"Faint? Well, not here. Do it somewhere else! 'Course you know this means a little more moola for you, but more importantly, you'll be more visible. Some of the big boys are sure to notice you. Did you know you're a real looker, Dodo?"

She stared at him as if not understanding, so he added, "I mean it, kid. You really look like Clara Bow. You know, the 'it' girl!" Wally raised his elbows and swayed his hips in a suggestive way but then stopped.

"Seriously, I'm really happy for you. I have a deep-down feeling you're going a long way, and this is just the beginning."

Dolores, as if frozen, stared at the director, until he said, "Go on! Get outta here! It's Saturday! Go out and have a blast! Celebrate! See you on Monday at the usual time."

She slow-walked to the dressing room in a daze but then questions bobbed to the surface and hit her all at once: *When? Where? How much? How long?*

"Shit! I should've asked him all that stuff."

She pushed her way through the jam of half-naked, jabbering girls. When she got to her station, she looked in the mirror; she was so elated she almost kissed her image. Then she thought of shouting out the good news for the other girls to hear, but she decided not to do it. *Forget it! They'll just get jealous.* In a rush, she pulled on her street clothes without looking again in the mirror. She wanted to get home to David fast because she couldn't wait to tell him the good news.

So now she was on the way home. It was a long ride: first the streetcar, and then a transfer downtown onto the bus, but it was okay because it gave her time to think.

You see, David? Just like I told you! All those hours of tap-tap-tapping my ass off on one chorus line after another. Now it's all coming together to mean something. Remember my first day at the studio when we saw I wasn't something special, that I was just another pretty face? I was just someone else who danced the Charleston and won a stupid contest just like dozens of other girls. Remember, David? Remember all the times I've bawled my eyes out thinking I was going nowhere fast? Remember, David, remember?

Dolores looked up the aisle toward the bus driver, anxious to get to her stop, when suddenly, her mother's face floated to the surface of her mind, accusing, dissatisfied, and looking down on what her daughter was doing. *Decent girls don't do what you're doing.*

Dolores shook her head to push away those words that cut so deeply, but no matter how much she tried, there they were, always popping up to ruin whatever she did.

It wasn't that she hated her mother; it was her words that were so tormenting. Yet this was what caused so many fights between her and David, and for this, Dolores was sorry because she knew it was her fault.

"David, one day I'll make up with Mama, and it'll be fine." She said this over and again, hoping to make things better.

In the meantime, however, she had to be careful because one day, her fame might get to be too much for him. She loved him above all things, even more than her dream of becoming a star, but did he know it?

She closed her eyes, trying to dig deeper into her heart, and she saw she caused David so much pain with her touchiness and constant squabbling. But now that this big break had come along, things would be different, and it was going to start right away, the minute she walked in the door when she got to their new place. When the subject came up—and it would—she would explain it all.

"Vignes Street!"

The driver's gruff voice snapped Dolores out of her trance. She jumped from her seat to the exit door in one leap, and she sprinted the couple of blocks to the duplex. Even if she was pooped, she ran trying to remember if theirs was the right or left door of the duplex. When she rushed in the front door, she found David sprawled out on the sofa, half-asleep.

"Wake up, David! I've got great news!"

He sat up, blinking; he had fallen asleep, waiting for her, but he was awake now that she was standing in front of him, smiling and waving her arms just as she did when she was dancing. He jumped to his feet.

"What's up, Lola?"

"David, we're going to celebrate tonight. Promise!"

"Yeah! But tell me what we're going to celebrate."

Slightly out of breath, Dolores took his arm and pulled him down to sit on the sofa next to her. Slowly, with a lot of care, a lot of drama, and a lot of detail, she told him the good news.

"I'm going to be on *that* chorus line, David! Rumors have been flying all over the place about the *Gold Diggers* movie, but honest to God, I didn't dream I'd be part of it. Can you imagine?"

David didn't know what to say; but because he saw so much joy on Dolores's face he, too, felt elated.

"This is what you've been waiting for, isn't it?"

"Yes! I'm on my way, my darling David." She used her most endearing words to speak to him, and he was moved.

"Well, let's begin our celebration."

David went to the cabinet where he had stashed a pint of bootlegged gin, took it and a couple glasses, and poured two shots.

"Here's to Lola, the famous movie star!"

"Here's to the dreamers!"

She raised her glass and then added, "And here's to you, David, and how far you've come."

They gulped down the rough-tasting liquid; he squinted his eyes, and she made a funny face, prompting them to break out laughing, pointing fingers at each other. It was their faces that David and Dolores laughed at, but most of all, it was because of pure satisfaction and confidence that they were on the right road; they were reaching dreams beyond what their old worlds could ever have anticipated.

"God, I feel like I'm going to blow up!" Dolores shoved her glass toward David. "Hit me again!" She mimicked a tough movie gangster, and they cracked up again. She gulped down the drink, this time, it went down smoother; she was getting good at it. Then they became quiet while the gin took hold, but they were thinking too.

"Do you wish your mother was here now?"

When David uttered those words, he realized it was a mistake—a big one, because he saw Dolores's face change from complete joy to a cold, stiff mask. She looked at him for just a second with narrowed eyes, but when she spoke, her words were a complete surprise.

"I don't know, David. Would it be a good idea? Would she understand and be as happy for us as we are?"

Stunned but relieved that he had been wrong, and that he had not stuck his foot in that mess after all, he refilled their glasses.

"I don't know, Lola. It's hard for me to tell."

"Then why did you ask about her being here?"

"I suppose it's because I think she'd be happy, and because I guess I'd like us to be a family. But honest to God, I don't want to hurt you, so I won't mess with it anymore. I regret the words that just popped out of my mouth."

Dolores chugalugged the shot of gin in one gulp; she was feeling oozy, and she liked the sensation. She put the glass back on the little table in front of them and signaled him to refill it.

"Listen, Lola, I'm sorry I brought it up. I'm sorry! One day I'll learn my lesson."

"No, my darling, don't say that. I'm the one that's sorry for hurting you so many times. Listen! I've been thinking about this and I've made up my mind to get together with my family—my mother and Sebastián especially."

Her words were beginning to slur a bit, but her smile was broad and sincere, so David poured another couple of drinks.

"Okay!"

They clicked glasses again, and he said, "In the meantime, let's drop the subject and have a good time. What do you say? What about if we dress up, go out for a good dinner, and then go dancing? It's Saturday, and the pier will be alive with happy people."

Suddenly, Dolores began to cry. Without warning, big tears rolled down her cheeks. Maybe it was the gin, or maybe she missed her mother, or maybe she was just so happy. Whatever it was, it soon passed. She sniffed hard, wiped her face, and smiled the way David loved.

"Okay! I'm starving, and in the mood to go dancing even if I have been hoofing all day long. And about the other thing, let me say that maybe I'll get together with my family someday, but not right away."

"Lola, I'd let my hands be chopped off rather than see you hurt."

He stretched his arms toward her with palms facing upward, as if ready for the chopping knife. His fingers trembled. She edged closer to him, close enough to put her head on his shoulder, and she wrapped her arms around his waist; she stayed like that for a while.

"No chopping of hands around here, darling David."

Her tears had stopped and maybe forgotten. David put his arms around her, and they stayed that way for a few minutes.

"Let's celebrate!" he said. "We have one another, what else do we need?"

"Nothing!" she said. "Let's go!"

CHAPTER TWENTY-NINE

The Big Crash

THAT YEAR, the roof caved in and the bottom fell out. It was the year the stock market crashed. It happened on the twenty-ninth of October, and the calamity that hit the country went on for over a decade. It was called The Great Depression.

From one side of the country to the other, it could be said the catastrophe hit overnight, even as people were planning their next party, or buying new shoes, or just snoozing. When they finally woke up to feel the earth shaking under their feet, they looked around to find their bank account had collapsed, and their savings were down the toilet. People really woke up when they got pulled into a foreman's office to hear, "Sorry, pal! I hate to say it, but you're out of a job."

CHAPTER THIRTY

1932

NO LONGER in contact with Dolores, the Gómez family survived the calamity by doing what they always did: They stuck together. Sebastián went into construction; he was skillful with equipment and in getting workers to put out their best. When the nightmare hit, houses and buildings were still needed, although on a smaller scale, so he kept his job, even if was at reduced wages, and he brought that money home to the family. The same happened with Pilar and Altagracia who managed to stick with the garment-making business. Their wages were also cut, and some weeks they didn't get paid, but whatever they earned, they brought it home for Cele's management. Even Héctor went out every day to rustle up pennies. He shined shoes, washed windows, delivered newspapers, all for nickels and dimes, and that was yet more money chipped into his mother's hands. She kept the Gómez household going despite the awful slump going on everywhere.

It was bleak for the family, nonetheless; just like it was with most of the country, and it meant a lot of sacrifice. Sebastián and Ofelia now had a baby, and that was an added burden, but the family got along, even caring for Valeria, and Ignacio, who didn't bring in money either. During those years, Cele managed to pay the light, gas, and water bills, as well as the rent and grocery charges; she had a knack with money. It was tough, but that's how they survived that nightmare from month to month; that is, until the letter came.

On that day, Cele could only stare at the sheet of paper Sebastián handed her because she couldn't understand what it said, except for the word *Repatriation*. She was sitting by Ignacio on the porch that late August evening, as she did every day, not to converse but to keep him company. It was a long time since Ignacio had retreated into the fog of hopelessness, and she accepted his silence; it was her way of dealing with his sadness.

She looked up at Sebastián as she returned the letter.

"What is this?"

"It came today, Mama."

He pulled up a chair close to her, took off his cap, draped it on his knee, and gazed out to the neighbors' houses before he went on. Cele saw right away he needed time to explain the letter.

"Sebastián, tell me."

He cleared his throat as he shifted his rump to find a better spot on the chair. It was obvious he was finding it hard to tell her what was in that letter.

"It says here we have to leave Los Angeles."

He pointed to the letter's beginning lines, trying to say it the best way he could, forcing his voice to be as calm as possible, but when he heard it, he knew his nerves were giving out, so he blurted out his next words.

"Not right away, Mama. We have a month to take care of things."

Dumbfounded, Cele stared at him; she thought her hearing was off.

"What do you mean...?" She broke off because she couldn't repeat his words.

Sebastián was just as shaken, but he tried to push back the terrible anxiety assaulting him. He knew he had to explain what the letter said, but at the same time, he needed to make it sound less of a nightmare than it really was.

"It's the government that—"

"That what?" She abruptly interrupted him. "What does the government have to do with our lives, where we live, stay, and why we have to leave?" She stopped to catch her breath. "Where are we supposed to go? This is our home, Sebastián!"

He was choked up and could only bob his head up and down in agreement. When he looked at Cele, she realized that his eyes were red, filled with tears, and that he was haggard. His hair was messy and tangled, and his jaw, always clean-shaven, was dark with a heavy shadow.

Sebastian's appearance jarred Cele, forcing her to stop asking questions, to stop talking, and she instead let out a sound that came from deep inside her. For his sake, she wanted to be calm, to see what was happening, so after a few moments, she told herself it must be a misunderstanding.

"I don't understand! The letter says we have to leave Los Angeles, but it doesn't say where we have to go." Then on second thought, she added, "Does it?"

"Yes, it does. The next line says that because we're Mexican, we must return to Mexico."

"No!" She exploded. "This is our home now, not Mexico!"

"I know! I know!"

After just a moment, Cele finally caught the terrible implications of what that piece of paper was saying. It was telling her they were foreigners, intruders, and that they had to return to where they had come from. Yes! She got that part! After all the years of migration, of backbreaking work under terrible conditions, in blistering heat and sand, of paying bills and taxes, of obeying laws, after all of that hardship, they were being thrown out. Cele got it! She saw the matter clearly! She knew what it was all about, but she didn't know why, and so she rejected the whole thing.

"Sebastián, they're not going to do this to us."

"There's nothing we can we do. It's the government that's ordering us to get out."

"We're going to fight! That's what we're going to do! Didn't we become citizens all those years ago? Even Valeria was born in this country, right there in Arizona. No, Sebastián! I'm not going to let anybody kick me out like a starving dog!"

"Can we prove we're citizens?"

Cele was so agitated she couldn't stay sitting, so she sprang to her feet to lean on the porch banister where she stood sucking in gulps of air. After a few moments, she straightened her apron, as if she was about to serve a meal.

"Yes! I have all our papers. Tomorrow, you and I are going to the city. I don't know which building or office, but we'll find the right place, and we're going to prove no one has the right to throw us out of our home." And she added with even more determination, "They don't have the right!"

Sebastián looked at her, and just then, he felt her fire spark him. He stopped being afraid; he changed, he felt ready to resist. He had more to say, however, so he reached up and nudged her back to her chair.

"You know that I come in touch with a lot of people at work. It's from them I first got wind that it's not only us. It's thousands of others like us, all Mexicans. Even from this street, families have already been deported to Mexico."

"Why, Sebastián? What have we done?"

"The rumor says los Gringos are sure we're stealing their jobs, that it's our fault their families are going hungry. We're eating up all the food, they say."

Cele leaned back and narrowed her eyes as she did when she caught on to a secret, or when she discovered someone lying. They were quiet for a time until one question, the most important one on Cele's mind, slipped out.

"If they throw us out, what will happen when Dolores returns and finds an empty house?"

As she said this, Ignacio unexpectedly stood up and made for the front door. He mumbled something under his breath, but before going into the house, he turned to look at his wife and son.

"I said we're going to be thrown out of this country no matter what we say or do. We have to prepare."

Without saying more, Ignacio went into the house, leaving Cele and Sebastián baffled. Just then, Pilar and Altagracia showed up at the front gate; they were back from work. They made their way up the porch steps, kissed their mother and brother, and then Altagracia began, as usual, to chatter. Pilar didn't say anything as she sat on the banister to listen. But then, because it was obvious that something bad was going on, Altagracia piped in.

"Why the long faces?"

Cele, in no mood to hold back, said, "Sebastián, show your sisters the letter."

Altagracia took the paper; all she had to do was read the heading.

"Repatriation? What does it mean?"

"Just what the word says, but we're not going to obey that order. This is our home, and we stay here!" Sebastián cautiously added, "But we have to prepare for the worst."

Altagracia was stunned into silence for a few moments, but then she became herself, "I think the whole thing could be fun."

"Altagracia, your brother and I have to talk. You and Pilar take care of our dinner."

Irritated by the girl's silly talk, Cele glared at her. She turned to Pilar and, with a nod of her head, signaled them to go inside while she and Sebastián stayed to make plans.

The next day, she and her son found the downtown office set up to deal with the thousands of displaced people, but it took hours for their case to be heard. As they waited, Cele, clutching under her arm the worn-out leather pouch that held the family's documents, patiently waited on line, watching the crowds that milled in and out of the hall. Faces turned in her direction, but even if there was no one she knew, she recognized familiar types from the many towns in Mexico and Arizona where she and her family stayed for months, and even years. Dark, leathery expressions looked back at her with eyes that asked, *Why is this happening?*

When Cele and Sebastian's turn finally came, the clerk at the window hardly paid attention to their questions and explanations. When she tried to show him the documents proving they were naturalized, the man gestured that he was not there to look at paperwork.

"That's not my department, ma'am."

It was useless. No matter how much Sebastián, at her urging, argued that they were legal residents, in the end, they couldn't get the agent to even take a look at those certificates.

"Mr. Gómez, you either take these train vouchers that guarantee passage for each one of you to Mexico, anywhere you choose in Mexico, or risk being picked up, slapped onto a bus, taken down the road to the border and dumped in Tijuana. Believe me, that's not where anyone wants to live. It's your choice! So stop wasting my time! There are a lot of people waiting behind you."

Exhausted and disillusioned, Cele's fire went out. She was left compelled to admit that she could not match the powerful force pushing her and her family out of their adopted country.

"Mama, if we don't leave now we'll be forced out sooner or later."

"Yes, Sebastián, you're right."

They returned home to begin its dismantling and doing away with their things. After that, the family packed suitcases with whatever they could carry, and Sebastián passed on his old truck to a neighbor in exchange for a lift to the train station.

On a foggy October morning two years after the stock market crash, Cele and Sebastián stood looking out from the caboose of the train as it inched away from Union Station headed for Mexicali. The Gómez family felt as uprooted and empty-handed as did the others jammed into the second-class coaches of that train headed in the opposite direction of their dreams. Years after having journeyed in search of a better life, the circle had come full turn for the family, and all they had to show for those years was the loss of two daughters, Hector's battered brain, and a father lost in a fog of depression.

CHAPTER THIRTY-ONE

AS THE train slowly rolled away from Union Station that foggy October morning, the Gómez family didn't know it, but at that moment, Dolores and David sat in their duplex a few blocks away, trying to find a way out of the mess they were in. After the market crash, they managed to keep their jobs for a time, and it wasn't until after months that the real slide began for them. Along with millions of others like him, David's savings were wiped out when his bank collapsed, but because he had stashed away some cash, he and Dolores more or less were able to keep up. He was quick to sell his car, and that brought in some extra money. They went back to using buses and streetcars to get around so they got along. The biggest help was that he kept his job at the Olympic Auditorium, and even if it was for less pay, David was grateful not to be sinking, like most other people.

But there were few distractions for them during the dreary months of the Depression, when she and David scrimped and saved just to stay in the duplex they had come to love. They couldn't afford to go out dancing or to restaurants anymore, but they dealt with this by telling each other that none of that was important. But it got harder every time to shrug off what was happening. All they had to do was look around to see signs of that creeping poverty. They saw people dressed in threadbare clothes, patched-up suits, and faded shabby dresses. Men stood on street corners peddling something or another, maybe overripe fruit or pencils. Little boys roamed streets asking, "Shoeshine, mister? Just a nickel." The scariest part was that people looked hungry, and the blight got worse each day.

It was during this time that a curious emotion began to take root in Dolores. It was silent and so deep that she hardly noticed it. She began to slide into a constant sadness, but because it was just a slight feeling at first, she ignored it, keeping it to herself, but the dejection was stubborn. It stuck and deepened, widened, and in time, inched its way up to the surface of her thinking, staying there nearly all the time, until it spilled out, angry and mean.

She often lost control of herself and picked fights with David, but because the bickering ended with making up and sex, he didn't pay attention to the overblown reactions to what he thought were silly happenings.

Time passed, but it was only a matter of time before the crash finally hit Dolores and David, and even though they knew it was coming, it still caught them by surprise; and it happened on the same day.

It hit him when his boss asked him into his office.

"Christ! David, it breaks my heart to say this, so I'll come right out with it. I have to let you go. Business for the Auditorium has been going downhill for a long time, what with our entries drying up, and all. There's no way out of it. We have to tighten up. You're not the only one. I'm losing my best guys. I can't even give you severance pay. Believe me, David, it breaks my heart!"

"I know, boss, I know."

David tried to pull himself together, but his voice, nonetheless, shook.

"It's really been good working with you, and who knows? Maybe things will get better soon."

"I wouldn't bet on it, pal, what with all the crooks running this country. We're fucked!"

David cleared his locker and left, but he didn't waste time before he headed for Shorty's Gym. He found Ricky talking with someone but stopped when he saw David.

"Hey, compadre! Where've you been? It's been a long time."

"I know, I know. How're you doing?"

"I'm okay. How's Dolores?"

But because Ricky didn't like small talk, he stopped in the middle of what he was saying.

"What's up, David? You look like shit!"

"They just let me go."

"The Olympic?"

"Yeah!"

"Oh, Jesus! Bad news! But it's all over the place. You know it, don't you?"

"Yeah!"

In fact, David was feeling close to desperate; thoughts of bills and payments were on his mind, so he got to the point.

"Is there a chance the gym can take me on?"

"Hmm!"

Ricky scratched his head and shifted his weight from leg to leg, obviously burning time.

"Let me talk to the boss. It depends on how things are going with business. Can you come back tomorrow early? I should know by then."

"Thanks, Ricky. See you tomorrow. By the way, have you seen Rosie?"

"Nope! She packed it all in when the diner closed. The whole family got in their jalopy and made for Oklahoma. Although I hear things are worse over there, so maybe she'll be back."

"I'll tell Dolores."

As this was happening to David, at almost the same hour Dolores, who thought she still had a job, was called aside by one of the trainers.

"I have bad news for you, kiddo."

She braced herself to hear the expected notice that the *Gold Digger* movie was suspended. But she was ready, knowing that she still had a job as an extra.

"You're out of a job."

"You mean on the *Gold Digger* movie, don't you?"

"No, kiddo. I mean you're out of a job. Period! The studio is closing down this section, and that means you and all the other chorus girls are out. So sorry."

With nothing else to say, the man left Dolores without giving her time to speak, or at least ask a question. It happened quickly and quietly, but the short exchange of words made the floor beneath her shake. She went to her locker without noticing that her companions were also feeling the same hurt; she walked by them without even sympathizing with them. Instead, she grabbed her things and headed home. She needed to be with David.

On the way home, David deliberately took time getting to the duplex. He was afraid to tell Dolores what happened, so he didn't hurry, but when he finally walked into the front room, he found her on the sofa, crying.

"What's up, Lola? Why are you crying?"

"Can't you guess?"

He knew right away. He sat close to her and took her in his arms.

"I don't have a job at the studio anymore," she said. "I've been kicked out, so I can't help with the bills. Maybe if I go back to the diner, I can get Ronnie to give me work."

"The place is closed, Lola."

"What?"

"I saw Ricky today. He told me."

She went back to bawling. Fat tears rolled down her face.

"What are we going to do, David? Maybe even your job at the Auditorium will dry up."

"It's going to be all right, Lola." He didn't have the courage to tell her the truth.

"We can't be afraid. If we stick together, everything will be okay."

David let time pass for the bad feelings to ease, but a few days later, he found Dolores with the eviction notice in her hands. She was shaken, but he wasn't surprised about the notice since they were two months late with the rent. The letter was blunt: "Leave the premises by next Monday!"

Although he got that part-time job at the gym after all, it wasn't enough to cover the rent and other bills for the duplex, so he knew they had to move to a cheaper place. David's heart ached, and it was made worse because he still had not told Dolores of his lay-off by the Auditorium.

The two dreamers sat in their front room looking at one another, mouths clamped shut. This whole thing was wrong; it wasn't supposed to be happening this way, not now that their dream had seemed so close. Yet there they were, stiff and speechless, surrounded by the shattered pieces of their dream, and neither one knew how to put it together again. David tried.

"I think we should go back to your family."

His words were a serious miscalculation because it lit a fuse buried deep inside Dolores. When it blew, it suddenly exploded. Her reaction was as if he had spat in her face or punched her in the belly. She lunged at him, arms stiff, fingers ready to claw, obviously intending to hurt him.

The blow-up was so sudden it stunned David, and all he could do was to hold down her thrashing, jabbing arms, trying to keep her from hurting herself and him. Holding on to her, he cried out, "Stop it, Lola!" But she only pushed against him. He held on to her wrists, but she twisted and turned until she got a hand free and managed to scratch his face so hard he yelped and pulled away, wiping blood off his cheek. It took him a lot of effort to hang on to his own rage because now he wanted to hit her.

"Goddamn it, Lola! Stop it!"

By now, Dolores had come loose from his grip, so she ran around the room, screaming, yelling out obscenities, throwing things at him. The barrage got worse; vases, ashtrays, planters, lamps, whatever she managed to grab smashed against the wall. All the time, David ducked and swerved because all those things were aimed at his head.

"Goddamn you! Goddamn you!" she screamed. "You blame me for this shit you got me into! It's not my fault! You're the one!"

"What in the hell are you yelling about?"

Now more baffled than enraged, David couldn't make sense of the outburst and even less of her cursing and accusations.

"All I did was mention your family! You're crazy!"

That word only pushed Dolores to more extreme frenzy.

"Crazy? Me, crazy?" She babbled. "You're talking of my father, aren't you? You're saying I've gone nuts like him, aren't you? Well, you know what? You're the one that's full of shit!"

"Oh, for Christ's sake, Lola, shut up! Just shut up!"

It was only when she thrashed around looking for more things to throw at him but found nothing that Dolores stopped the madness. She stood bawling, howling, panting, coughing, trying to catch her breath; she was choking, and her face was turning blue, then she suddenly crumpled to her knees, her hands clamped on her belly. David saw she was in trouble, so he dropped to the floor and crawled to her.

"Lola, no more, no more!"

He took her in his arms and cradled her close to his chest. "Breathe, my darling, please breathe!" He smoothed her hair, caressed her forehead, and kissed her eyes. "No more, darling girl! You're making yourself sick."

He rocked her gently; right there on the floor of that wrecked dismal front room. He did it until his own rage retreated, giving way to the growing fear of losing the woman he loved above all things.

Anguished, he pleaded, "No more, Lola! Please!"

Conflicted and unsure of what had caused her violent reaction, David nonetheless clung to Dolores; he held on to her as if an unseen power was about to swoop down out of nowhere and snatch her away. He didn't know why or when she lost her way, but he knew that she was slipping away from him, and he didn't know where to turn for help. What he did know was that he wasn't going to let go of her.

After a while, Dolores recovered some kind of calm, and he more or less cleaned up the mess while she slumped on the sofa.

Then David said, "C'mon. Let's try to sleep."

Once in bed, she drifted off, but he found it impossible to sleep; instead, his mind raced.

He knew he couldn't live without Dolores, and he also understood that he desperately needed help to keep her. So risking another outburst, he did the only thing he could do. The next day, he went in search of her family to ask for help, but he did it behind her back.

CHAPTER THIRTY-TWO

HE FOUND the house, but it was empty; no one lived there anymore. A neighbor came out to ask why he was peeping in the windows and pounding on the front door.

"What's up, buddy? What're you snooping around for?"

"I'm looking for the Gómez family. They live here."

"Not anymore!"

"What? Where did they go?"

"They were shipped back to Mexico."

"What?"

"Yeah! You heard me right. They packed all their shit into their jalopy truck, bags and all."

"Why?"

"Jesus, man, where've you been? It's happening to most Mexicans, at least those the patrol can't round up and snag."

"The whole family?"

"Sure enough. The crazy old man, kids, even the dribbling dummy, all of 'em got packed up and sent away."

When the man saw David's distress, he went on, "Hey! I'm sorry to give you the bad news. Were they your family?" The man scratched his head. "You don't look like one of 'em."

David mumbled, "No," and walked away.

Later on, he was careful not to tell Dolores what he found out. He was afraid the news would unhinge her again, and he thought that this time, she had good reason for going crazy.

After this, the downward spiral for David and Dolores became unstoppable. Her depression deepened even more until in a short time, its unspeakable sadness boxed her in, isolating her from her surroundings, and even from him. For his part, anxiety and powerlessness to save Dolores filled David more and more each day.

CHAPTER THIRTY-THREE

DOLORES LOOKED around the room where she was sitting on a narrow bed with rusty springs that squeaked every time she moved. David was away; she was alone. It was late November, and it was nearly dark. It wasn't raining, but it was foggy and drizzly.

The room was a bleak small place. It had a hand basin built into the wall where there was water, and there was a window that opened out toward the bridge. Their suitcases were on the floor because the room didn't have a closet, and the toilet was down a dark, cluttered hallway. No matter where they went, the hotel stank; it was filled all night with drunken voices and slamming doors, but the room cost only a dollar a week, all they could spare, so that's where they landed after their eviction from the Vignes Street duplex.

She and David had gotten the room in that run-down hotel on Santa Fe Street on the west side of the river near the base of the Sixth Street Bridge. When they walked into the hotel, a bald, skinny man at the front desk slapped a key on the grimy surface.

"One buck up front for a week. No questions, no conditions. Just mind your own business."

How long had they been there? Maybe it had been a few days, or maybe weeks. Dolores couldn't remember, but as she waited for David, she wasn't thinking of the squalor. She was lost in thought remembering her family and their travels to a better life. She pictured the places they had lived in, some just garages, others shabby rooms in broken-down houses.

Her thinking turned to her brothers and sisters, and she wondered about them. What would happen to Héctor, with his bashed-in brain? And Pilar? What a mystery she was to Dolores, so quiet, so uncomplaining, never speaking, as if all she wanted in life was to melt into the woodwork.

Maybe she can't stop thinking of how she killed the guy that raped Mama. Maybe.

Dolores mumbled, and her mind jumped from thought to thought, trying to explain why she didn't want to go back to her family, but after a while, she had to admit that she was ashamed. After all, she was the daughter who was supposed to be the famous movie star, the one who would visit them, all dressed up and driven in her chauffeured limo filled with presents. She was the one who was going to buy them a house, not a chickenshit little frame thing but a real house with a bedroom for each one, and a parlor and kitchen, and even a maid to help Mama. But now, that wasn't going to happen.

Dolores sat in that dreary room, muttering and even gesturing as if there had been an invisible listener. Then, as she did most of the time, her thoughts abruptly turned away from memories of her family to look only into herself, wondering why her life had become so dismal, so hopeless.

Thoughts of becoming a star and the joy that dream had given her still thrilled her. She thought of how real it had been, and how she never doubted she would reach being someone special. It had been so close she could almost touch it! Instead, she turned out to be a fake, an empty thing, a do-nothing trapped in a box with nowhere to go, fighting every day to get rid of that stinking misery crushing her heart. Dolores understood that when her dream died, she died too. Not her body, but inside, in her head, in her guts; and the pain was unbearable.

She closed her eyes to think of David, and how much she loved him, and how he loved her. She knew he was down to his last coins, and that when he left her it was to bring back food. He didn't fool her; she knew he stole the loaf of bread, the pint of almost-sour milk, and what about the sandwich she knew he snatched off a vendor's cart? That was the day he returned panting and sweating. "I needed exercise," he had said, but she knew he was running from someone chasing him.

Dolores slumped on the bed and rolled over on her side with her knees pressed against her chest. She had tried to find a job to help him, but there was nothing; everything had dried up. Now she found herself trapped in this stinking room where she had given up trying to fight the squalor surrounding her. She even stopped washing her face or combing her hair days ago.

Trance-like, she thought over and again, *What difference does it make?* And she went on, relentlessly picking at the rage burning in the pit of her belly, although her mind tried to drag itself out of that mire. Her thinking struggled to stretch upward to where there was light, but it was useless. Instead, her spirit slithered back into that ocean of mud inside her, and each time, the darkness closed in on her again; each time, it hurt even more.

Just like Papa! I'm like him! I know now the misery he's felt during all these years. It's my punishment for having caused the mud inside him.

Sometimes David and his stories helped her out of that sadness. When she asked him, he told more about himself than he had since they met. He talked about his days with his family, when he was just a boy, and then of being shut up in an orphanage. He talked of the old woman and of her wisdom and vision and her death in a church built by people long ago. David even told of how the old woman knew when and where she would die, and that she talked of it from the beginning of their journey.

Just as captivating for Dolores were David's descriptions of churches and temples, and men dressed in robes and turbans. But he talked, too, of lost, homeless people that traveled from place to place in search of shelter and food. "Just like what's going on in our streets," she muttered. "Just like what's happening to us."

Dolores, too, again told David about herself because he asked her, although her life didn't have the same feeling as his. "Tell me about your life, Lola," and she did it, beginning with her dimmest memories. A lot of it was repeated, but this time, she didn't hold back anything.

She opened up about her sister Esperanza, how she ran away with some lowlife and disgraced her family. "Which explains why my father went nuts."

But David wasn't shocked, as she thought he would be. He merely put his arms around her and murmured, "It's all right, Lola, everybody's got something stuck down deep."

All that talk between them held her imagination, although it was mostly repeated, nothing new. But it only captured her attention for just a little while because no sooner did they fall into silence than her mind again tumbled back into the blackness of a depression so intense that she thought she was suffocating.

Rolled up on the squeaky bed, Dolores's eyes drooped and then closed, but she wasn't asleep; she was thinking.

"I want to die. Right now! In this room that stinks of rats and cockroaches, now is when I want to die. But how will I do it? Jump out the window? We're on the second floor. I'd only break a leg, maybe both, then what would happen?"

Dolores surrendered to those dismal thoughts because they gave her a curious escape from the pain of depression, so she often gave in to thinking of dying, almost every minute of the day. She wanted to die, to take away the pain. She knew it had to be suicide, but she couldn't do it by herself. She needed help.

On that day, she was in the middle of those thoughts when David returned empty-handed and shaken. The bald skinny man at the desk told him they had to get out before the week ended because they hadn't paid a week's rent. David was scared and felt lost. He had tried everything to come up with the money, including the pawnshop, so now even his watch was gone, along with the two dollars he got for it.

"Lola, sit up! Let's talk."

She opened her eyes, but her mind was still stuck on the thought of death. It took her a moment to focus on his face, and she saw it had lost its beauty. His cheeks were drawn, covered with a black shadow, and his hair was shaggy and oily. He was about to say something, but she interrupted him.

"When you told me about the old woman's death, you said she predicted it from the beginning of your journey, and that she knew the time and place where she would die."

David, taken by surprise by her tone but especially by what she was saying, frowned, trying to make sense of it. "Yeah, I said that, but what's that got to do with what's going on with us?"

"How did she know the place and even the time of her death? How can anyone know that much?"

"Christ, Dolores! I don't want to talk about that, not now. I have something more important to tell you."

"Nothing is more important! C'mon, David! How did the old woman know when and where she was going to die?"

"I suppose she was mystical." He exhaled with impatience. "In fact, I know she was mystical. She knew things like that. She was almost a mind reader."

"I don't think so, David." Dolores shook her head hard. "The old woman knew when she was going to die, and there's only one way she could know it. She planned it."

Intimidated, David jerked away from Dolores.

"What makes you say that?"

"Because it's the only explanation! She wasn't a creepy crystal ball reader. She was a flesh and blood woman who knew what she wanted. She planned her death, and she did it to herself."

David felt the room spin and then rock until it made him dizzy. He looked at Dolores, and in that instant, she caught the truth in his eyes. She had put her finger on the heart of his long-kept secret. He realized she had hit on what really haunted him, even more than the murder of the Turk, more than all the indecent, vile acts of his life. It was what he had never dared to speak of.

"She planned it, but she didn't do it alone, did she, David?"

He didn't answer; he only pulled away from her, his mouth set in a rigid line. He knew in that instant where Dolores was going with her questions.

"She didn't do it alone, did she, David?" She repeated the question, this time, in a stronger voice.

"No!"

"You helped her."

"Yes!"

"How did it happen?"

"I don't want to talk about it. It's the past."

"Tell me, David! Please!"

After a few moments, he thought, *Why should I keep the truth from her? She knows already.*

"It happened at the foot of Queen Isabel's altar where Zepyur took off her shawl, handed it to me, and said, 'David, press this to my nose and mouth until I depart.'"

"Did you do it?"

"Yes."

"And then?"

"She departed. Afterward, I took her body from that chapel and didn't stop until I reached the hill where I built a fire. The rest I've told you."

"Do you regret it?"

"No. It's what she wanted."

They were quiet; only the splatter of raindrops on the windowpane broke the silence. David was shaken; he crumpled on the bed with his arms wrapped around his head while Dolores caressed him.

She murmured, "I am Zepyur." She didn't say more, but he understood and replied, "No! I can't do what you want me to do."

"David, I'm leaving, with or without your help."

"This ugliness will pass, Dolores. We're young. Let's live! There's a future."

"Not for me, and I'll do it when I choose. Maybe I'll do it when you're not here, or some other time when your back is turned, or asleep. Maybe I'll jump off the bridge or out of a window. Whatever, I'm going to do it, but I need your help. If you did it for the old woman, why not for me?"

"No! You're not thinking right. Life is beautiful. Why should anyone want to end it?"

"Because it stops the pain!"

He didn't answer because he couldn't, and after a few moments, she went on.

"With or without you, I'm leaving."

He leaned against Dolores and wept because he knew what she planned was irreversible. He knew that she was sick; that her heart was broken as was her mind. He got to his feet.

"I need to leave you for a while."

"Where are you going?"

"I won't be long. Wait for me."

David left that sad room to walk along streets littered with dismal sights of homeless people living in doorways and cardboard boxes. They were silent hungry men and women, some sat in pairs, others huddled in clusters, but most were gaunt solitary figures sitting and waiting for what would never arrive. It hit him that when Dolores was gone he would be just another empty shadow clinging to a dirty wall.

I'll be just another one of these miserable stiffs.

The rain became heavy, but he drifted through those streets and lost track of time; was it minutes, hours, or even decades? Time slipped by as David walked aimlessly, thinking not only of Dolores and himself, but also remembering that he had already experienced a similar destruction when he was a boy. He thought of the mass killings of his family by the Ottoman Turks, and he remembered how he had been uprooted and cast adrift in search of shelter.

As David walked the streets of a ruined Los Angeles, it hit him as never before that he had been robbed of his family, and that he had walked through life alone, without a mother or father or brother or sister. He had grown up alone without a grandfather or grandmother or aunts or uncles. He had lived alone until Dolores came to him!

David abruptly stopped walking; his eyes riveted on the muddy concrete, and his thoughts cleared.

Although I've survived a solitary life once before, I can't do it again, not without Dolores. If Zepyur chose the time and place of her death, so will I.

"I can't live without you," he said to her when he returned. And when she didn't say anything, he went on. "We'll do it together."

They didn't say more; the pact was sealed. They stretched out on the squeaky bed without taking off their clothes or shoes. Wrapped in each other's arms, David and Dolores slept.

EPILOGUE

THE DREAMERS left that squalid room. They walked the short distance to Sixth Street and then turned up toward the bridge. It was only noon, but November brings darkness early in the day to Los Angeles. Heavy clouds loomed over the eastern mountains, and to the west, fog slithered off the Pacific Ocean's sleek surface. It was a damp gray day, so they clung close to one another.

They walked slowly, arm in arm, like lovers do on a balmy spring lakeside day, or on the seashore; they chatted about things they had already said many times over. She told again of her girlhood days in Arizona, how she and her sisters passed their days, and of how playful Héctor used to be before he was crippled. She reminisced about their life in Mexico, and she even remembered the Revolution.

David told more about Zepyur. He recalled his days in the Kasbah of Constantinople, and his mentor, Maestro Abenray. They chatted about trivialities, but their minds were on what they had agreed.

"It will be in a car, Lola." David explained, "I can control it."

"But we don't have a car anymore."

"I'll steal it."

He said it casually, and she didn't think more of it.

When they reached the midpoint of that high bridge, they stopped and leaned on the barrier to gaze down at the river, now swollen with rain, its black current glistened with silver-tipped ripples. David's attention was drawn to the orphanage on the river's east bank, its gothic dormer windows and turrets so tall they seemed to be reaching for the glowering sky.

"Look! An orphanage like the one where I lived when I was a boy."

But Dolores was looking elsewhere. She was staring down at what was under the bridge, along its mud banks where homeless people huddled under raggedy pieces of canvas, old blankets, or pieces of cardboard. Here and there were small campfires, but wherever there was space, it was littered with trash and human waste. Over there, on the far embankment, two men fought over a piece of cardboard.

"I can't go on living in this world, David."

Distressed, David took her hand and pulled her away toward Boyle Avenue, but as he did it, he looked at her and saw how wasted she looked; he remembered they hadn't eaten in a long time. At the same time, he felt her grip on his arm weakening, so he led her to where the bridge ends on Sixth and Boyle, and there he found a bench where they sat to regain strength. Then he happened to see a man not far away selling fruit. David stuck his hand into his pocket and found a nickel.

"Wait here."

The man was selling apples. He was dressed in what must have once been an elegant suit, but now it was worn out and frayed.

"How much?"

"Two apples for a nickel."

"Give me two!"

As David turned toward Dolores, a little boy jumped in front of him.

"Mister, can I have a bite out of one of your apples?"

The boy was emaciated, barefooted, and his face showed signs of hunger. David remembered that same look on his brother's face before he died of starvation. The ridge above the eyes protrudes, the cheekbones and teeth stick out, and the mouth is rimmed by a sickly purple. He remembered, too, his own pangs of hunger, when he would have done anything for a crust of bread.

David handed the boy one of the apples.

"Take it!"

The boy's eyes widened in disbelief, but at the same time, he greedily snatched the apple from David's hand and skittered down the street, shouting, "Thanks, mister! Thanks, mister!"

When David returned to Dolores, he fumbled in his pockets, looking for a pocketknife, and then, as if preparing the apple for a picnic banquet, carefully carved it, feeding her one thin slice at a time while he licked the fruit's juice from his fingers. After a while, he said, "Look, there's our car." He pointed at a Ford parked along the sidewalk. It was shiny and beautiful despite the rain.

"Let's do it."

Dolores didn't hesitate and got to her feet, although slowly; strength was rapidly draining out of her. The car wasn't locked, so they climbed in. He reached under the dashboard and fiddled with the wires until the engine turned over. He pulled away from the sidewalk, U-turned, made a right on Sixth Street, and headed east.

David cruised away from the orphanage, his speed regular, just enough to keep up with the flow of traffic. After a couple of minutes, where Sixth turns into Whittier Boulevard, he pulled over to the curb but left the engine idling. He turned to look at Dolores; the question was in his eyes. She returned his look and murmured, "Yes!"

He pulled the car away from the curb and headed toward Euclid Avenue, the boulevard's highest point, all the time gaining momentum. At the crest of the hill, he stomped down hard on the throttle. The V8 engine kicked in, and the car careened downhill out of control with nothing to stop it.

Printed in the USA
CPSIA information can be obtained
at www.ICGtesting.com
LVHW091234300923
759526LV00002B/425